FOURKEEPS

EVER AFTER DUET, BOOK 2

JAYNE RYLON

ABOUT THE BOOK

The Ever After duet concludes with *Fourkeeps*...

When you're wealthy, you're used to getting what you want.

But when what you want is a gorgeous woman to share a lifetime—and a really big bed—with you and your three best friends, it can be a tough sell.

Ford, Brady, and Josh are determined that nothing will keep them apart. Not Kari's past or the asshole who keeps threatening their future.

One night with her was amazing, but it could never be enough.

This time, they're playing for keeps.

Fourkeeps is the conclusion of the Ever After Duet, and should be read following *Fourplay*.

ADDITIONAL INFORMATION

Sign up for the Naughty News for contests, release updates, news, appearance information, sneak peek excerpts, reading-themed apparel deals, and more. www.jaynerylon.com/newsletter

Shop for autographed books, reading-themed apparel, goodies, and more www.jaynerylon.com/shop

A complete list of Jayne's books can be found at www.jaynerylon.com/books

1
———

Ford Westbrook rubbed his stomach through his dress shirt. The motion didn't calm the growling and churning anymore. "Hey Brady, didn't you say Kari was bringing some dinner over to the office?"

Blinking, Brady Arman looked up from the closing remarks he'd been drafting for a high-profile case their law firm was handling. He studied the clock as if it didn't make sense. "Yeah. Is that right? It's really *eight* already? She thought she might get here by six. I did tell her to take her time, but..."

Their other partner, Josh King, shook his head. "Are you saying she's over two hours late? That's not like her."

Ford paced the office carpet. "Something's up. Either you can call her and check on her or I will."

Brady frowned. "I don't want to go full barbarian on her. She quit her job here for exactly this reason. She didn't want us nosing around in every corner of her business."

"Normally I would agree with you," Josh said to Brady. "Except she's always on time. If something came up, she would have at least texted you to let you know her plans had changed."

"That was when she was our employee," Brady argued. "Now she's our girlfriend...I guess. Big difference. We can't act like we own her or we risk losing that privilege too."

"I get it. I do." Ford nodded. "But sorry, you're outvoted this time. We've waited long enough."

"You call her," Josh told Ford, then turned to Brady. "It's okay, she'll understand we're worried for her. And honestly, I'm hungry enough to eat that damn case file by now. If she's not coming, I've got to order something or run down to the hotdog cart on the corner."

"Damn, you *are* desperate." Brady frowned.

"Hey, if their special seasoning is the taste of burnt roaches, then I like bugs every once in a while," Josh joked. It didn't really help cut the tension escalating between the three men, though.

Ford hesitated just long enough for Brady to reluctantly agree. "Okay, fine. Do it. But if she's pissed, it's your fault. And I don't plan to stop seeing her because the two of you have a falling out."

"I'm happy to take the blame so long as she's all right." Ford nodded then pulled his phone from his pocket and dialed. None of them were experienced at serious relationships and this one was far more complicated than most. It was going to take some work and some getting used to, all of which he was prepared to handle.

Of course, he couldn't do that if Kari wasn't around or even taking their calls.

His face fell. "Voicemail."

Brady looked like he might have puked if his stomach

weren't empty. "What if something really happened? And I...*oh shit*."

Josh put his hand on Brady's shoulder and squeezed.

Brady whipped out his own phone and tapped the screen a few times before putting it to his ear. He looked up at Ford and Josh in horror. "Voicemail."

"Maybe I'm the lucky one tonight?" Josh didn't sound hopeful, but he grabbed his cell too. He dialed, then paused before pulling it away from his face. He stared at it shock for a moment before saying, "Hello? Who the hell is this? Where's Kari?"

The silence that followed was one of the longest of Ford's life. Before Josh even finished listening, he was motioning for Ford and Brady to follow him. He dropped his case notes and sprinted toward the elevators, his loosened tie flapping behind him.

What. The. Fuck!

Ford and Brady followed without question. Screw the trial. Forget their work. If Kari needed them, that was most important.

"Is she okay?" Ford asked as he smashed the elevator button and flicked his gaze to Josh.

Josh didn't answer right away, though sweat began to dot his brow, making a knot settle in Ford's guts. The acid burning in them had nothing to do with hunger and everything to do with cold dread.

"Josh!" Brady shouted. "What the hell?"

He mumbled to the person on the phone, "Thank you. We'll be right there."

"Where are we going?" Ford asked.

"St. Mary's Hospital," Josh responded, his normally chipper and enthusiastic tone terrifyingly devoid of emotion.

"Why? Is Kari okay?" Brady grabbed Josh's arm.

He shook his head then buried his face in his hands. "They don't know yet. She was brought in nearly three hours ago. Hit by a car. She's still in the trauma center under some sort of protective order and they can't release information over the phone. We're lucky that nurse answered at all. I got the feeling she wasn't really supposed to do that. Because we all called at once, she probably figured Kari's family was freaking out."

They were.

Freaking out. And her family. They were both.

In that moment, Ford knew it absolutely. If—no, *as soon as*—he could tell Kari, he would do just that. It was time they admitted they were playing for keeps.

Brady was one step ahead of Ford, his fingers flying over the screen of his phone as they rode the elevator downstairs. "Bronson is bringing the car around. He should be out front in two minutes."

"Fuck!" Ford punched the embossed paneling of the elevator. He'd only felt this helpless once before, when they'd realized that Kari had been assaulted by Marty right under their noses.

She'd already suffered so much. She didn't deserve this too.

"This is my fault," Brady groaned as they piled onto the curb. He bent over, his hands on his knees.

"It's not." Ford shut that shit down fast. "It was an accident."

And he would make damn sure that if the driver had been reckless or intoxicated or distracted, they would pay for hurting the woman he was coming to love.

That thought hit him so hard, he might as well have stepped out into traffic himself.

Sure, he'd always respected her. Appreciated her skills in the office and the beauty even her stark wardrobe couldn't obscure. He'd looked forward to their easy conversations. But when she'd unraveled in his arms the other night while his partners gave her the tiniest taste of what they were capable of and she'd absorbed it all plus reflected it back, he'd known deep down.

She was meant to be theirs.

No one was going to take that from them.

"I should have insisted that Bronson drive her here." Brady groaned and swayed.

Josh put his hand on Brady's back. "That's not what she needs from us. That wasn't what she wanted. You respected her choices, which is the only way this will ever work. If we get the chance…"

He trailed off, clearing his throat as if considering any other possibility was too painful.

Because it was.

Tires squealed right then as Bronson took the corner out of the garage nearly on two wheels. The guys didn't wait. Together they bolted toward him and piled inside when he screeched to a halt.

No one spoke again as they flew through the city on the blessedly short drive to the hospital.

It was hard enough to breathe, never mind form coherent thoughts.

Until he saw Kari, nothing would be right in Ford's world. From the grim expressions on Brady and Josh's faces, he knew it was the same for them.

2

J osh stood behind Ford, spine straight, arms crossed. He backed Ford up while his partner did what he did best, even if it meant Ford roamed into asshole territory. The guy confronted the nurse who was doing a hell of a job blocking them from finding out any shred of information about Kari.

Meanwhile, Brady had planted himself shoulder to shoulder with Josh, and Bronson had their back. He'd refused to stay in the car, insisting on helping out in any way possible. He had a soft spot for their girl, and Josh couldn't say he minded.

Hell, he understood exactly how Kari could get under a man's skin. Make him care in ways he didn't think himself capable of.

"You misunderstood me. That wasn't a request. We need to see Kari right now. And if you need to clear that with someone, talk to Dr. Patel. Just do it quickly. Please." That last bit was ground between Ford's clenched teeth.

Of course, Ford was referring to their friend Ansh, who was the youngest neurosurgeon ever appointed to the board of directors of St. Mary's. The one who had convinced them to donate millions of dollars to fund the expansion of the critical care unit at this very same facility. They'd never dreamed they would be in need of those services themselves, though.

Ansh had also been a guest at Ford's thirtieth birthday party on their yacht, where they'd first begun to explore their attraction to Kari. He must have seen the way they looked at her and would understand their desperation now that she'd been hurt.

The trauma center shift manager sniffed and rolled her eyes, but she reached for a red, hardwired phone on the wall nearby. In less than a minute, which seemed like an endless delay, they were on their way down the hall.

The woman's spine was ramrod straight as she blasted them with curt instructions. "Don't disturb her. She'll wake on her own, when she's ready. Be quiet. Don't touch anything. Make sure your phones stay off. And don't you dare harass my staff. Let them do their jobs. They will take care of her as best as they're able. Better if you don't interfere."

"Thank you," Brady said softly. "We appreciate everything you've done."

The woman looked over at him with a hint of a sad smile. "You're welcome."

"So what can you tell us about her condition?" Josh clenched his fists, trying to prepare himself for what he might see when they rounded the corner into a secure ward. "All we know is that she was hit by a car."

"She was fairly lucky, as things go." The nurse sighed. "It seems like she took the brunt of the impact to her hip then rolled up the hood and over. That's actually how they teach stuntmen to do it. If she hadn't...things would have been much, much worse."

"Fuck!" Ford barked.

The nurse stopped short. "That's not quiet or calming, is it?"

Josh put his hand on Ford's shoulder and left it there long enough to feel the steely muscles beneath his fingers melt as his friend forced himself to relax. "I'm good. Keep going."

They continued their journey through too-bright halls toward a set of blue doors. The nurse swiped her badge and admitted them to a bay of six private rooms with support staff at the center. She pointed to the first one on the left. "She's sleeping. They gave her some pretty strong painkillers and ran a full battery of tests. Long story short, she's going to be okay."

Relief washed through Josh. Something wasn't adding up. Apparently Brady had the same questions in mind.

"I guess I'm a little confused. If she's mostly unharmed, then why is she being isolated? And why the ban on visitors?" Brady wondered, his eyes slitted.

"The police asked for her to be kept quarantined until they've had a chance to interrogate her. If she wakes, don't speak to her about the incident until they can get an untainted report."

Ford held his hands up, palms out. "Okay, that makes sense. We're lawyers. Believe me, no one wants to figure out what the fuck happened and who's responsible more than we do."

"Perfect. If you mess this up, it's on you. No one can say you didn't understand the consequences and I won't be held responsible." The woman softened some and relented, opening Kari's door to usher them inside. She left them there and pivoted on her heels toward the station inside the ward. Probably to warn her coworkers about the three pain-in-the-ass rich men who'd been allowed to bend the rules.

It wasn't often they wielded their wealth or power like a weapon. But in this case, Josh was fine with using any advantage they had.

Bronson peeked in over their shoulders before saying gruffly, "I'll be right here, waiting for the cops and making sure no one interrupts you."

"Thanks." Josh nodded before slipping past the guy who'd become like a father to them. He hated to admit it, but he felt better knowing Bronson was there in case they needed him.

They shuffled toward the bed, the machines, and the small, pale form tucked beneath the stark white sheets. It must have punched the other guys in the gut as much as it did Josh to see Kari like that, so frail and helpless. Both because they hadn't kept her safe that day and because it made it all too easy to imagine what she'd gone through...before.

His legs shook and threatened to give out.

Brady shoved Josh toward a shitty plastic chair beside the bed. He crumpled into it and reached toward Kari's hand, stopping short of holding it for fear of disturbing her. His fingers shook in the air between them.

"I don't know if I can do this," Brady rasped. He might have left if Ford hadn't physically prevented him from going by blocking the narrow path around the hospital bed with his broad shoulders.

"You didn't let her down earlier. But you will if she wakes up and you're not here. Get your shit together, for her," Ford ordered.

"I should have picked her up. Or at least insisted she let Bronson drive her home." Brady groaned.

"You're not responsible for this," Ford said for the millionth time.

A nurse appeared just then, maybe to check on Kari, but probably to make sure her visitors were behaving themselves. The young guy with a smattering of tattoos sized them up. He scanned from man to man to man, pausing on Josh. "You good?"

"I will be if she will be," he croaked, though the room had started to spin.

"Step aside." The nurse gestured to Ford and Brady, shooing them out of his way as he came in for a closer look. Josh swiped self-consciously at the sweat on his forehead, noticing his skin was clammy when he did.

Bronson was glaring in from the hallway too. Everyone was staring at him, which didn't help the situation. They were here for Kari. Not him.

Except he drooped, feeling sort of faint just then.

Josh would permanently lose his man-card if he passed out at Kari's bedside.

He lurched to his feet, or at least he tried. The nurse was there, along with Brady, to brace him and settle him back into the daffodil-colored bucket seat.

"Whoa. You're not diabetic, are you?" The guy whipped a blood pressure cuff off the wall and slapped it on Josh.

"No."

"When's the last time you ate, dude?" the guy asked.

"I don't remember. I had a couple donuts for breakfast. And maybe a leftover one for lunch." His bad habits were starting to catch up with him, like Ford always lectured they would.

"Your blood sugar is crashing." The nurse looked to Ford and Brady. "Help him out for a second. I'll be right back."

"You want me to hit a vending machine for some snacks?" Bronson asked.

"Nah. There aren't any near here. We don't usually allow guests in this wing." The guy was already halfway to his station. "I've got some extra pudding and apple juice for the patients, though. Hang on."

It wasn't more than thirty seconds before he was back, handing Josh a plastic cup that felt ridiculously small in his fist. He guzzled the liquid despite the fact that it looked like piss, then shoveled the entire cup of pudding in his mouth in two plastic spoonfuls.

"Chill out and you'll feel better in a few minutes," the nurse told him, backing off so Josh could salvage a shred of his dignity.

"Thanks for keeping him from busting his thick skull when he toppled over," Ford said to the nurse, clasping his hand. "And for taking care of our...of Kari."

"No problem. But I actually just came on shift. I haven't had a chance to review her file yet." He strode to the door and grabbed a set of papers before flipping through them. He paused, then looked up, really studying her pale face for the first time. "Oh damn. She's the girl from YouTube, isn't she?"

"YouTube?" Brady parroted.

The nurse nodded. "That was some scary shit. How that guy shoved her. Did they figure out who it was? I'm surprised he's not in a room next door with the way you guys are hovering around her. I'm not judging, you know. I'd do the same if she were my loved one."

Ford looked at Brady, then at Josh, then at Bronson. To

anyone else he would have seemed calm. Josh could see the fire raging inside him when he asked, "What exactly are you saying?"

The nurse froze and blinked. "You didn't know about that? Ah, fuck. I should keep my mouth shut."

"No, I'd like to hear more." Ford got quieter and quieter, which any sane person would see as a clear warning sign of his impending explosion.

"Don't get me written up." The nurse held his hands out. "Please. I need this job. I have a daughter..."

"We're not going to get you in trouble," Brady promised smoothly. "Just help us figure out what's going on."

"Have you had your phones off the whole time you've been here?" The nurse frowned. "I know it's against policy, but maybe you'd better take a look. I can call the cops in too. They want a statement from her anyway. That's the best I can do. Sorry."

He started retreating out the door. Before he'd vanished, Josh already had his phone in hand and had pulled up YouTube. He didn't have to search. The horrifying video was right there.

#1 in *Trending*.

Somehow he didn't think Kari would be thrilled about this kind of notoriety either.

Shit.

"I recognize this vlogger. Marsden McPhadden has a cult following." Josh scowled. "Hell, I think he even has a side gig with some of the major news networks. It's no wonder this is blowing up."

Ford, Brady, and Bronson gathered around as Josh rotated his phone to make the video larger, then hit the play button.

A young guy with trendy spiked hair and a faded rock band T-shirt was talking into the camera as he filmed himself riding an electric skateboard around downtown. He was facing the same direction Kari would be pointed if she left her office and headed home. And in fact, yes, that was her in the background, over Marsden's shoulder.

It was surreal to watch her like that, oblivious to whatever sick turn the day was about to take. She grinned, swinging her purse along with a glossy black bag while she walked. Josh couldn't help but smile back at the image of her, deliriously happy on her way to meet up with them even if it was for a shitty dinner at the office.

Until he saw it. The moment she'd realized something was wrong, even if he couldn't tell what it was at first. She stiffened and her stride stuttered. That hadn't been what caused her to trip. It was hard to make it out in the crush of people surrounding her, but there was someone trailing her, walking too close. Someone in a black coat. Someone who seemed familiar even if he couldn't see the guy's face. It was something about the way he moved.

No, that was crazy, wasn't it?

Whether or not it was the person Josh suspected, Kari thought it was him too. She spun on her heel and stumbled backward toward the traffic zooming by. Josh cringed, wishing he could reach into the screen and grab her. Save her.

The guy scaring the shit out of her could have done that. He was right there in front of her as her arms windmilled and she tried to right herself. When it seemed like she might tip forward onto the sidewalk again, his hand smashed between her breasts, propelling her into the street.

"Son of a bitch!" Brady yelled as she took a yellow cab to the quadriceps.

"Oh Jesus," Bronson muttered.

Ford said absolutely nothing. It freaked Josh out almost as much as watching Kari tumble over the vehicle and flop onto the pavement, inches from the screeching tires of the car behind the cab, which barely managed to stop before running over her prone form.

"Am I crazy or was that..."

"Marty Schone. I'm going to kill that motherfucker!" Ford roared.

From beside them, Kari made a strangled gurgle. She pushed mostly upright in bed on shaky arms with a horrible wail. Though slurred, her concerns were easy to understand. "Marty? Where?"

She scrambled like some kind of uncoordinated, cave-dwelling insect that had been blasted with a beam of intense light. Though she wasn't very effective due to the drugs in her system, she squirmed toward the headboard in a grotesque effort to melt into the nearest crack and hide. Josh's heart broke. She should never have to be afraid.

He'd thought she was recovering. Now...

He didn't blame her for her instinctive terror. Neither did he know how to make it go away. But he swore then and there that he'd do his best for her. To help her recover and keep her from ever being hurt again.

Josh looked at Ford then Brady and saw the same fierce protective light shining in their eyes.

That and something else he couldn't quite identify. Maybe something like longing, or gratitude that she was still with them at all. Anger too, of course. And self-recrimination. It was a powerful jumble of feelings he'd never experienced before.

It was in that moment that he truly understood the complexity of emotion behind one tiny word and wondered how it could mean so many different things all at the same time. This, he thought, was love.

It might not have been as pretty as he once imagined, but it was unbreakable.

Or at least he hoped so.

3

Confusion reigned. Kari flinched away from Marty, but the ground was squishy, not rough like pavement or steely like the honking car she expected to find beneath her searching hands as she crashed into the street. What the hell?

Where was she?

Gentle arms came around her and a familiar voice teased her from her panic. "Kari, it's me, Brady. You're safe. We're here with you. Calm down, okay? You could hurt yourself worse."

Immediately, she went slack in his hold. "B-Brady?"

"Yeah. I've got you." He stroked her hair, making her shiver as she realized it was true. If he was there, she was going to be okay. He wouldn't let anything happen to her. "The guys are here too. See? Ford and Josh are right next to the bed."

"Bed?" She reached out blindly and someone cradled her fingers in their much bigger hand. Ford, she thought, based on his slightly rough grip. "Josh?"

"Right here, Kari." A light touch on her forearm joined

Ford's clasp on her hand and Brady's reassuring hug.

She snuggled in tighter to their warmth and protection even if she hated seeming weak in front of them. "What happened?"

"Why don't you think about it for a minute? We don't want you to say anything yet, though. Or talk about it with us. Police officers should be here any moment and we'd like you to tell them exactly what you remember, okay? It's important." Brady rocked her as he gave her instructions, ones that started the gears in her mind turning again.

Kari shook her head, wincing as it began to throb. She buried her cheek against Brady's chest and breathed deep of his expensive cologne. Having the guys surrounding her gave her the strength to recall walking home and what had come after.

A tear slipped from the corner of her eye. She shifted to swipe it away. No. She would not cry over that asshole again. Never again.

"Excuse me. I'm Detective Bonner with the OSPD. We need to speak with Ms. Hill."

Reluctantly, Brady peeled his arms from Kari. She sighed, nodding up at him when he eased back a tiny bit. She needed to do this. Unlike last time, she wouldn't stop until Marty paid for what he'd done to her. With their support, she could face it and conquer it. Keep him from ever putting her in this position again.

Kari smiled weakly at Ford and Josh, then turned toward the officer.

She spilled everything, from her phone conversation with Brady to the route she'd walked and how she'd first noticed Marty behind her. To her surprise, he didn't think she was crazy. The man nodded, took notes, and didn't interrupt once while she told her side of the story.

However, Ford had gone stone-still.

"You believe me?" she asked, and hated the part of her that was certain everyone would think she was nuts. Again. Like the night at the restaurant. Or the morning after Marty had assaulted her at the Christmas party.

"It would be hard not to with that video to corroborate your statement." The cop's mouth was a grim slash across his serious face.

"Video?" Kari tipped her head, wondering if she was hearing right. "Like from a surveillance tape?" Maybe she'd gotten lucky and there was a traffic camera at that intersection or something in a shop window nearby that had recorded the incident.

"No, ma'am. We haven't been able to find one of those yet. We're still checking, but there was a man vlogging for his YouTube channel nearby. He caught...most of what happened to you in the background of his video."

"That's amazing!" Kari perked up. "So you have enough evidence to go after Marty this time?"

The cop cleared his throat and looked busy writing something in his notepad. Ford cursed.

Josh stepped closer to her. "You can't really ID him from the video alone. I believe you. Hell, I knew who it was right away, even before you told us. But it was more about the way he walks and stuff. You can't see his face clearly."

"In court..." Ford trailed off as if he couldn't bear to say the rest. They would know better than anyone if what they had was good enough for a conviction.

"Yeah. It leaves more wiggle room than I would like," Brady confirmed, shaking his head.

Kari thought she might be sick. Not because of the dull thud in her thigh, which was probably all sorts of ugly colors beneath the bandage she was sporting. No, it was the familiarity of the person who'd sabotaged her that had her blood freezing in her veins.

The officer glanced around the room then. "So help me understand. Why would this asshole go after her now if the original incident with him happened a while back and he was never formally charged for it?"

Ford stepped forward. "First, I think he might have been stalking her for a while. You can talk to the manager at La Bonne Vie. Kari and I were there about a week ago. Someone banged on the window by our table. I didn't see him, but Kari thought it was Marty. I'm sure now that it was."

"Did anyone at the restaurant try to find him?" the cop asked.

"Yeah. There was no one hanging around by the time they checked the street." Ford cursed again.

"So again, what's been happening that's setting this guy off? Making him bolder? What does he have against Ms. Hill?"

Brady pinched the bridge of his nose. "I got a call from another firm about Marty last week. Asking for a reference. I was honest with them about the issues our firm had with him and could not recommend him."

"Shit." Josh scrubbed his hand through his hair. "I fielded a couple calls like that myself."

"I had the same conversation no less than five times over the past two weeks." Ford smacked his fist into his opposite palm hard enough that Kari flinched. "I didn't say anything to my partners because it's...well, a sore subject."

"I see." The cop made more notes. "So he's probably getting desperate for a job at this point. Maybe running out of money. Developing resentment that could easily be aimed at Ms. Hill if he blames her instead of his own actions for his termination."

"This bastard is dangerous. And he's not going to touch Kari ever again." Ford leveled a glare at the police officer so intense and icy that Kari cringed. A groan slipped from between her lips as her leg cramped and her head pounded.

"I think she's had enough." Brady stepped between her and the officer. "Is there anything else you need at this time?"

The cop flipped his notebook closed and shook his head. "This is enough to get started. I appreciate your cooperation. Please let me know if you think of anything else. We'll be in touch."

Bronson was there, seeing the man out and shutting the hospital door quietly behind them. Kari was alone with Ford, Brady, Josh, and all their emotions.

Her vision unfocused.

"You okay?" Josh asked. "Do you need me to call one of the nurses?"

"I'll be fine." She knew that with them by her side, it was true. This was entirely different from the last time she'd survived an attack by Marty on her own. "Can you get me out of here? I want to go home."

"By *home* do you mean your apartment?" Ford responded in a tone of voice that matched his raised brows, making his answer to that suggestion clear.

Brady frowned. "That doesn't seem like a good idea."

"I'm exhausted and I just want to sleep in my own comfy bed instead of this thing." She banged her knuckles on the hospital bed. "I don't like all these strangers around, either. Please."

Ford looked like he was about to argue when Josh stepped in. He wasn't authoritative, but entirely too rational to argue with when he made a proposal. "Let's be honest. None of us want to let you go right now. Our place is very secure. The building has a lot of wealthy residents and our penthouse has the extra precaution of the private elevator. There are cameras all over the entry and lobby leading up to the elevator. And I'm positive Bronson would be willing to sit out his shift at the front desk. No one is getting in without us knowing. Even if they did, our place has a safe room that's damn near impenetrable. Let us take you home...to *our home*."

Why did it sound like he was implying it was her place too?

"It's where you belong," Ford added, as if that was the final argument.

Brady glared at him, then joined forces with Josh, persuading her with calm rationality. "We have several guest suites. You can have your pick. You don't have to do something you're not comfortable with or bunk with one of us if you come."

"Of course you're welcome to, if you'd rather," Ford said, earning himself glares from his partners.

Kari couldn't help it. She cracked a smile at their antics. Their reassurances helped, truly. She wasn't quite ready for anything more intense than she'd already lived through right then. "Yes, okay. I'll go home with you. And take you up on one of those guest rooms. Does it by any chance have a massive soaker tub?"

"Yes. Yes, it does," Brady reassured her, and reached out to squeeze her hand. "Thank you. I promise you won't regret it."

"I'll talk to the staff." Ford strode toward the door.

Kari nodded. Her eyes prickled. Thank God they wouldn't shuttle her to her place and drop her off. Sure, that was a better alternative than being stuck in this hellhole, but truthfully she wanted to be with them. Now and always.

"Be right back." Ford marched out of the room with such purpose she knew that no one would stand in his way. She hoped he was half as serious about claiming her for their own.

"Where are my clothes?" Kari looked around. A clear plastic sack draped over the back of the chair next to her bed. All she saw inside it was the glossy black bag from the lingerie shop. The one she'd filled when today was supposed to be about things a hell of a lot more fun than a hospital stay.

"I'm guessing they cut them off you." Josh winced. "Did you go shopping on your way home? Just wear whatever this is that you bought."

Kari tried to stop him, but she was groggy and he wasn't.

Josh fished out the satin and lace. He held it up to admire it. Brady eyed the sexy underwear, his jaw dropping.

Just then Ford reentered the room. His stride hitched when he took in the garment dangling from Josh's fist. "Damn, I leave for one second and you guys get up to that?"

Kari laughed again, surprising even herself. Despite the pain and uncertainty swirling around them, these guys could make her do that. Her heart fluttered. She relaxed for the first time since she'd heard Marty's sinister whisper behind her on the sidewalk.

"My mother always told me to have clean underwear

in case I got in an accident. Somehow I don't think this is what she had in mind, though." She shrugged as if it was no big deal that she'd obviously been intent on seducing them when she'd bought the get up.

"I hate Marty even more because he fucked this up for us." Brady gritted his teeth.

"Don't worry, I'll still wear it for you...someday." Kari winced as she peeked at the bruises she could already see creeping up her leg above the edge of the bandages.

"Damn straight you will," Ford said as Josh put the lingerie back in the bag and patted it lovingly.

"I'll ask Bronson to go get you some clothes," Brady offered.

"The nurse said they're going to do a couple more checks on Kari. If there are no issues, she'll be approved for discharge tonight." Ford glowered as if preparing to fight anyone who said otherwise.

Kari was glad to have someone to stand up for her even if she knew she was capable of doing it herself. This was so much...easier.

"Thank you." She leaned against Josh, who hovered close to the bed.

"You don't need to thank us, Kari." He hugged her. "We're here for you, and we always will be. That's what family is for, right?"

Brady and Ford nodded as if Josh hadn't just set her world on fire.

Was that what they thought of her? Did they feel the same way she did?

For now it was enough that they were near. She relaxed into the pillows and let herself rest while the doctors did their thing. The sooner she was out of there, the better she would feel.

4

Kari stumbled. Her arms flailed as she searched desperately for anything to halt her momentum. There was nothing. She was going to end up in the street. A flash of yellow filled her peripheral vision.

The crunch of her body rolling up onto the hood of the vehicle was followed by a razor-sharp, white-hot pain that lanced through her upper thigh. For a split second, she glimpsed the driver's face. It looked as horrified and shocked as she felt.

A scream ripped from Kari's throat. She tried to get up, but she couldn't. The pain was too intense.

"Hey, hey. Kari! You're okay. It's all right. It's only a dream."

Kari thrashed some more until she realized she couldn't move because she was tangled in the softest and most luxurious sheets she'd ever slept on.

A shadowy figure stood nearby, naked from the waist up. She could make out his features in the glow from a light in the bathroom. That's right, he'd left the door cracked when he tucked her in earlier. "Yes, sweetheart. That's better. You're here. With me, Brady. At our house. Josh and Ford's house too. Okay? Is it all right if I come closer?"

Tears blurred Kari's vision. She couldn't speak, so she put her arms up.

Brady whispered his thanks to her or to some invisible force, she wasn't sure which. Either way, he crossed to her in two giant strides and sank onto the edge of the bed. He gathered her gently, carefully, into his arms and stroked her hair.

When he began to rock her back and forth, she clung to him and the comfort he offered them both.

"I was so scared," she cried. "I fucking hate that. Hate being afraid. Am I going to freak out every time I cross the street now? It's bad enough I can't go into alleys on my own anymore or enjoy parties like I used to or even have a damn drink to calm my nerves. That bastard. How much more is he going to take?"

She didn't say it, but she wondered if something might have developed between her and the guys sooner if they all hadn't been fucked up by what had happened at the office Christmas party. How much time had they wasted?

"I'm sorry, Kari. I was terrified too. I still am." Brady wasn't too macho to admit it. She appreciated that about him. "I couldn't take it if anything happened to you and now—not once, but twice—you got hurt when I should have been looking after you."

"No. That's not true." Kari tried to shake him. Too strong to budge beneath her trembling arms, he stayed still while she rattled herself. "You're not taking this on. You didn't do anything wrong."

"It feels like I did. When I saw you in that hospital

room. Unconscious..." He buried his face in her hair. "Son of a bitch. I'm sorry."

"Brady?" she whispered, aching to take away his pain like his presence alone did for her.

"Yeah?"

"Kiss me. Don't stop until I forget about yesterday and six months ago and all the things I'm afraid of." On the growing list was ruining her budding relationship with him, Ford, and Josh. They were the brightest part of her life right now and she needed them...*him*...more than ever.

Kari tugged Brady closer. He didn't resist. It was sort of like it had been with Josh and yet, different too.

Because Brady wasn't playing. He was dead serious. Yet so damn careful, she knew without words how precious she was to him and how shielded she'd always be, here in the circle of his arms. So she didn't resist when he leaned forward, pressing her back against the mountain of pillows on the ridiculously plush bed they'd lent her.

It felt like sleeping—okay, well, making out—on a cloud. It was easy to forget the harsh realities of everyday or the ache in her thigh when he sucked her lower lip between his and nipped it.

Kari whimpered.

Brady moved far enough away to ask, "Did I hit your leg?"

She hated the space between them. Needed to feel his heat and weight grounding her. She wrapped her arms around him and hugged him tight, until he slid back into place, their chests mashed together. "No. I don't feel that at all when you're touching me. Distract me some more."

"How much more?"

"A *lot* more." Kari figured she would have to deal with any repercussions later. Right now, she needed him. Not wanted—although that was true too—but *needed*. He eased the tightness in her chest and chased away the lingering wisps of her nightmares.

"Are you sure?" he double-checked.

She nodded then wriggled until she could walk the oversized T-shirt Josh had lent her up her thighs and hips. When it bared her pussy and the dip of her waist, Brady froze.

At least for a moment or two. Then he dove between her legs to inspect the flesh she'd revealed to him. He petted her stomach, not seeming to care that it was softly rounded instead of chiseled into abs. She was nothing like the swimsuit model he and the guys had been rumored to be fooling around with most recently.

In fact, he seemed to like the way her skin felt against his fingertips. Brady kept caressing her, over and over, following every line, dip, and curve of her body as if committing them to memory. His rapt attention turned her on, making her feel like a goddess when all she was doing was lying there, enjoying herself.

Kari buried her fingers in his hair and rubbed his scalp. His eyelids lowered, making him look even sexier when he shot her a smoldering stare. He turned his head to place a kiss on her wrist, right above her pounding pulse, before returning his attention to her torso.

He gently pried her hand loose from the cotton and took over, lifting it over her ribs. It took forever, because he insisted on blanketing every exposed inch of her skin in butterfly kisses. It was as if the thought of someone hurting her pained him too, so profoundly that he had to reassure himself that every bit of her was intact.

Kari didn't plan to rush him. She wallowed in the liquid heat he inspired with his mouth, tongue, and the warm wash of his breath. Here, in their hushed togetherness, she couldn't imagine anything negative intruding. She felt truly safe for the first time in months.

Ironic that it was on the day she'd been attacked, yet again.

Brady healed wounds that were too deep for stitches. He was like the world's best medicine being pumped through her system. Serious, yet kind. Patient. Everything she needed right then.

"Are you okay?" he asked softly when Josh's T-shirt was hung on the bottom swell of her breasts. "Is this too much?"

He paused to swipe a tear from her temple. She hadn't even realized they were rolling from the corner of her eyes and into her hair as she stared up at the ceiling. "No."

Brady stopped and began to get up from the bed.

She hooked her good leg around his waist to keep him in place. "It's not too much. In fact, it's not enough. I still need more. It feels so good to let go."

"Then give me everything. I'll take care of you this time." He kissed her neck then, nearly making her spine arch right off the bed. "You don't have to worry about anything when you're with me."

It was pretty much the most intoxicating thing anyone had ever promised her. And because she knew him—knew how responsible and detail-oriented, how kind and hardworking he was—she believed it was true.

Kari surrendered. She went limp beneath him, flinging her arms out and spreading her legs wider so he could settle more fully between them. He wasn't in any hurry. Not rushing toward some destination. Rather, he let them both enjoy this exploration, wherever it took them and whatever they discovered about each other along the way.

"Yes." He licked and nipped a path down her neck to her collarbones, which were visible in the wide neck of Josh's shirt.

That thought made her hesitate. Long enough that Brady noticed. "If you change your mind, say so. You won't hurt my feelings. I'm here to do whatever you want me to do...or not do. You never need a reason to say no to me, okay?"

Maybe not, but she had two of them to think about.

"What about Josh and Ford?" She sighed, already craving the feel of his lips against her again.

"They went back to the office to hammer out some details on our case and draft a request for a delay to give the judge in the morning."

"Because of me?" she groaned, some of her passion fizzling.

"No, because of Marty. None of this is your fault, remember? Plus it's good experience for Cooper, who's assisting them in my place." Count on Brady to spin this into a positive.

Kari gasped then. "Wait. What about Andi?"

Brady grimaced, though he never stopped caressing her, toying with the edge of the cotton at her collarbone and tracing imaginary swirls up her neck. "She's on lockdown at her apartment, worried for you and pissed that her guys wouldn't let her out to see you, mostly. Reed and Simon are there with her. So far it seems like Marty is blaming you for losing his job and being unable to get a new one, even though we all know his blackmail attempt on Cooper over his relationship with Andi was the real reason he got fired."

"Oh, thank God." Kari felt like shit that she hadn't considered sooner the possibility that Andi might also be in danger. If it meant her friend was safe, she'd gladly take the brunt of Marty's focus and attention.

"You don't have to worry about any of that tonight, Kari. It's just you and me here. No one else can get inside if we don't let them, remember?" He said it as if he was talking about inviting guests or warding off intruders, but she realized he was referring to her thoughts. Her fears. Her ability to let phantoms run her life. She didn't intend to do that anymore.

Kari nodded. She got what he was saying and even knew what she wanted to do about it. Mostly. "Do you think...? Will Ford and Josh be mad if we...?"

What were they doing exactly? How far would they venture together?

"If we make love?" he asked, as if afraid to say it out loud in case she wasn't on the same wavelength.

He shouldn't have worried about that. Releasing her lip from between her teeth, she nodded again. "Yeah. That."

"They'll know I'm the luckiest man in the universe tonight. I don't think they'll be upset. They care about you and they want whatever is best for you. Somehow, right now, that might be what I'm good for. To help you. Please, let me make you feel better."

Kari sniffled, then decided she'd had enough of tears for one day. His generosity moved her. "Am I dreaming again?"

A wide smile graced Brady's face then. "No,

sweetheart. You're wide awake. I mean, have you ever had a dream that felt like this before?"

This time he wasn't playing around. Brady trailed his hand down from her neck, between her still-covered breasts, then over her stomach. He brushed her mound, making her rock toward his touch. When he cupped her pussy, pressing the heel of his hand over her clit with precisely the right amount of pressure to make her moan, she practically saw stars.

No, that was definitely too vivid to be a dream.

Just the stuff of one come to life.

Under ordinary circumstances, she might have rolled to her knees, straddled him, and taken her time getting to know his body as well as he was coming to know hers. Not this time.

"Do you mind if I just lie here and let you do...well, whatever it is you're about to do?" She wiggled her fingers at her boobs and lower.

"Not at all." He smiled, slow and sexy.

"Have at it." She couldn't say what it did that he waited for her to give him the clear green light before advancing.

"Tell me if I hurt you," he murmured as he peeled the shirt off her. He kissed every single bruise and scrape he came across, making them seem inconsequential in the face of the rapture he gave her.

"You won't." She hoped she wasn't lying. Not that he'd ever harm her physically, but emotionally? If this went astray, she wasn't sure she could recover.

"I'll do my best not to. Ever." He admired her, laid out in front of him. Both with his gaze and his caresses, which made her feel worshiped. They put her in a floaty daze.

So it surprised her when, after a few minutes, he nudged her shoulder and rolled her onto her side before lying behind her. He took her injured leg and gingerly raised it so that it was draped over his own. To be honest, she was on enough painkillers that she didn't feel any discomfort. Or maybe that was his touch working its magic.

Kari gasped when his naked chest pressed to her back —skin on skin.

He was so much more muscular than his lean form in his crisp shirts might have had her believe. His cut form molded to her perfectly.

"You fit me just right," he said into the darkness. The firm length of his cock aligned itself along her ass, nudging her as he shifted his hips.

Would that be true when he was inside her too? She couldn't wait to find out.

Brady adjusted behind her. Fabric rustled as he did something—shoving his pants down, she assumed, when suddenly the thick heat of his erection lay against her ass.

"Damn it," he growled. "I need to get a condom."

He shifted, and Kari thought she might die. The last thing she wanted was for him to leave her alone in this giant bed.

"No, you don't. I mean, not for my sake." She winced in the darkness.

"You're on birth control?" he asked quietly.

"Yeah, ever since Marty... It just seemed like the smart thing." She was so glad he couldn't witness the stain on her cheeks then. "I've been tested a bunch too, since...you know...but if you're not comfortable with that, I totally understand."

"Kari...don't." He kissed her cheek. "I would never think less of you because of what that scumbag did. I hope you know that."

"I do, but sometimes it's easy to forget." She shrugged one shoulder.

"Let me remind you then." He reached between them to align his hard-on with her opening. Brady notched the tip at the entrance to her body, then pressed forward, fusing them together bit by bit. His cock worked inside her pussy, reminding her just how long it had been since she'd welcomed someone inside her.

It didn't hurt, not exactly. It felt like the aftermath of going to the gym after a decade-long hiatus. She'd forgotten she even had some of those muscles. Brady reawakened them, from the inside out.

Kari gasped.

He froze. "Are you okay? Is this okay?"

"So fucking okay," she groaned, and squirmed in his embrace, trying to force him deeper.

He chuckled, then resumed his movements. Before long, he'd advanced as far as he could.

Brady held her in his arms and slid into her from behind, hugging her to him as he joined their bodies. The only thing she regretted was that she couldn't look into his eyes as he filled her and made her entire being hum with satisfaction. It blew her mind to be joined with him like this.

Kari tipped her head to the side. Brady groaned and covered her lips with his own. He was so gentle. So kind and forgiving. It was everything she needed right then.

Tonight Ford might have been too intense.

And Josh might not have been serious enough.

Brady was perfect. The perfect man. The perfect lover.

He rocked his hips behind her, fucking her slowly. Every slide of his cock in and out unraveled her further. She melted all around him and in his arms. Her eyes widened when he shifted. The blunt head of his cock rubbed against someplace magical within her.

"There?" he asked, whispering in her ear.

"Mmm..." A soft moan was all she could muster in response when he did it over and over, perfecting his approach until she thought she might swear off sex with anyone else for the rest of her life.

Except that brought Ford and Josh to mind.

Her pussy squeezed Brady's stiff shaft as she imagined what they would think or do if they were in the room—no, in the bed—with them right now.

Ford wouldn't hesitate—he'd enter her, squeezing beside Brady's cock, stretching her until she could accommodate them both. Josh would kiss her, distracting her from any temporary zings of discomfort. Kari could almost sense their presence.

Brady groaned. He cupped her breast in his palm before running it down her stomach and toying with her clit instead. "I need more hands."

"If Ford was here, he'd help." Kari couldn't believe she'd said it. Her thoughts spilled out. With Brady she was comfortable enough to say whatever came to mind without censoring herself.

"Fuck yes, he would." Brady's next thrust was a little less steady, a little more forceful. "And Josh would give you something to do with your mouth."

Kari licked her lips, imagining sucking him while Ford and Brady sandwiched her between their pumping bodies. That much heat and muscle and man surrounding her might be enough for her to OD on testosterone.

Or maybe to lose herself entirely. She could finally be unburdened from her doubts and fears long enough to fly.

That thought coupled with Brady's skilled lovemaking shoved her to the precipice of pleasure. She flung her hand down and grasped his, squeezing his fingers as tightly as her pussy hugged his cock.

"You're ready?" he asked as he stroked her faster and deeper.

"Yes."

"Thank God." He groaned, then nipped her neck. Only enough to let her know how much he needed her too. His finger rubbed across her clit at the exact right angle to set her off. Her back arched, pressing her ass closer to his. Her breasts thrust forward.

Again she imagined Ford there, his chest plastered to hers where only cool air was now, maybe even as Josh watched or joined in.

As she came, she called Brady's name. Her second moan was Ford's and then Josh's. They might not be there in person, but they were always on her mind. And in her heart.

As she settled back to earth, Kari wasn't sure if Brady would feel differently than he had in the heat of the moment. If she should be embarrassed that it was so obvious she'd been thinking of more than just him while he did such a phenomenal job of pleasing her.

He held her tighter as he poured himself inside of her, his hips twitching with each pulse of his orgasm. "Yes, Kari. Yes. Soon. Soon we'll all be together."

He grunted as he made that promise, emptying himself entirely. His breathing was heavy as he recovered. His face buried in the crook of her neck, his arms tensing around her periodically as if to make sure she was still there.

"Brady?" Kari cleared her throat.

"Yeah?" He kissed her temple, then snuggled her close to his chest.

"Why was it you?" Shit, that sounded horribly rude. She was glad it had been him with her. But had they known he was the right person for tonight too? Or had it been something else? "I mean…"

"I know what you mean." He hugged her. "I couldn't leave you. Not again. Not after…"

It was then Kari fully understood he had needed this even more than she had. She refused to feel bad about bringing him ecstasy and comfort. Relief. Even if she should probably have waited for Ford and Josh too, so they could take this step together.

No, tonight she could only do what it took to survive.

There would be plenty of time for regrets in the morning.

5

K ari was going nuts.

It was bad enough that she'd woken to an empty bed. If the pillows on the opposite side of her hadn't been rumpled, she would have started to believe she'd dreamed the night before. Well, that and the inarguable impression Brady had left on her body. It felt entirely different from the stiffness in her joints and the soreness in her leg, which actually wasn't nearly as painful as she'd imagined it might be.

Maybe he'd released enough endorphins in her to mask some of the effects of her unfortunate run-in with that taxi. Or perhaps she'd simply been extraordinarily lucky.

Kari shivered as she thought of the video she'd snuck a peek at on her phone. Things could have been so much worse. And sitting around alone in this enormous empty penthouse wasn't helping to distract her from the situation.

She'd already tidied her room, returned an email from her boss—who'd seen the infamous vlog and told her not to come in to work for at least a week—cooked herself a meal from the ridiculously well-stocked fridge, napped and napped again, then caught up on some trashy TV. If she didn't talk to someone soon, she'd be bonkers by the time the guys got home. Who knew how late they'd be, if they even made it back tonight. She knew the case they were working on was high-profile so she didn't want to bug them with messages or calls that weren't important.

Chewing her nails, she paced the cavernous living area, dining room, and kitchen. Even the gorgeous view was curtailed by gloomy gray clouds and a cold drizzle that had been coming down for hours. When she couldn't stand being isolated a moment longer, she grabbed her phone and tapped Andi's icon in her contact list.

Before it even had a chance to ring, the call went through. "Kari! Oh my God. Are you okay?"

"I'm still here." She shrugged despite being alone. All things considered, that was a win.

"Shit. You must be so fucked up right now." Andi sighed. "I'm so sorry that bastard is still harassing you. The guys are going to find a way to stop this for good. You know that, right? Even Cooper is working on it with them. They're not going to stop until Marty goes down."

"Huh? Oh, him. Yeah." Kari was kind of surprised that wasn't top of her mind at the moment. Regardless of everything else, she'd believed Brady when he said she was safe here, locked in their tower. "Truth is, I think I have bigger things to worry about."

"What could be worse than that?" Andi got quiet, as if she was tucking herself somewhere private to give Kari her full attention.

"If I do something to screw up things with Ford, Josh, and Brady." Kari had known terror the day before. So she was positive that's what even thinking about losing the guys triggered within her. It probably wasn't healthy, but suddenly the stakes seemed higher than this apartment, which made her dizzy as she stared out at the drop beyond her feet, the ground undetectable through the clouds.

"*Something* like..."

"Having sex with Brady last night when Ford and Josh were at the office." Kari sank into a chair and rubbed her stiff leg.

"Wow. I wouldn't have thought you'd be up for that. But..." Andi cleared her throat. "People deal with trauma in a lot of different ways. If that's what it took to make you feel alive and release some of your tension after a near-death experience, I'm sure the other guys will be fine with it."

"That's basically what Brady said last night." Kari couldn't stop thinking about the time before, though. When things had blown up after Ford and Brady discovered she'd made out with Josh the night of Ford's birthday party. It had caused a huge fight between them.

Something she never wanted to be responsible for again.

"Do you trust him?" Andi wondered. "Because what you four are doing is going to require a hell of a lot of that."

"I do." Kari didn't hesitate for a moment.

"So chill out." Andi was chuckling then. "You're going to be fine. All four of you. If you feel the need to be fair, then make tonight all about Ford and Josh. I'm sure they won't complain."

Kari thought about the glossy black bag that one of them had placed, just so, on the center of the dressing table in the guest room they'd invited her to stay in. It would make her feel more confident to be wearing that than these extra-baggy sweats Josh had donated to her. She'd had to fold over the waistband about a million times to make them stay put.

"You know what? You're right." Kari smiled for the first time that day. She wanted to take charge of her life. That meant she had to quit letting circumstances rule her emotions and shove her down paths she might not choose herself. It was time she started being proactive. "Thanks, Andi."

"Ford and Josh can thank me." She laughed. "Tell them I like sparkly things for Christmas."

"Will do."

"Kari, seriously, I'm so glad you're okay. It wouldn't only be the three of them who would miss you if something happened." Andi was uncharacteristically serious when she admitted it. "And...uh... I feel like it could very easily have been me that psycho was pissed at and obsessed with since he got fired because of the situation with Cooper and me."

"I guess I'm just lucky." Kari didn't want her friend to feel a moment's guilt about that. "Look, Marty is obviously losing it. Just because he hasn't done something to you yet doesn't mean he won't try. Stay close to your guys. Please."

"Oh, trust me. It's not like they're going to let me out of their sight anytime soon." Andi groaned. "In fact, Reed texted me saying he's waiting in the lobby to drive me home and if I'm not down there in five minutes he's coming to find me."

"You'd better go then." Kari grinned, imagining him stomping through their cubicle farms in search of his fiancée.

"And you better prepare yourself too." Andi confessed, "He also said Ford and Josh are on their way to see you. Cooper and Brady are taking their turn holding down the fort at the firm tonight."

Kari glanced at her reflection in the plate-glass window, suddenly finding it lacking. Her hair was snarled, her face was pale, and her clothes looked frumptastic instead of endearing. She didn't have a lot to work with, but she figured she would do her best to look like the strong, desirable woman she wanted to be by the time they arrived.

"Gotta go," she mumbled as she did her best to climb the ornate circular staircase without a wince.

"Have fun!" Andi was laughing as they disconnected.

Kari figured she should start with a shower. To be honest, she hadn't taken one earlier because she didn't want to wash away the feel or scent of Brady on her body. When the warm water from multiple showerheads hit her muscles, she wished she had soaked in the mammoth jetted tub for a few hours.

By the time she emerged from the steam, she was feeling a million times better. Good enough that she looked at the bag sitting on the dressing table for only a second or two before lunging for it. Self-doubt wasn't going to stop her anymore.

It took her a few tries, and a peek at the image in the online catalog, to arrange the straps and lace panels in all the right places. When she finally had it right and checked herself out in the full-length mirror, she figured they were a helluva good distraction from the scrapes and bruises that marred her skin.

Kari gave her hair a quick blow dry, upside down, then flipped it over. It looked wild and untamed, just like she felt. It was a freedom she hadn't imagined possible until recently. The pride pumping through her veins made her feel powerful. Gave her back some of what had been taken from her. Never again would she let someone else have that kind of hold over her.

Hopefully, Ford and Josh would appreciate her transformation.

Glancing at the clock, she figured they should arrive shortly. So she made her way back downstairs and thought of the best way to state her case. She climbed onto the massive table that sat directly in front of the hallway leading from the entryway and arranged herself like the most decadent centerpiece she could image.

She'd barely settled into place when a knock came at the front door, followed by familiar voices. Ford called, "Kari, it's just us. Ford and Josh. We're coming in, okay?"

"Yup." More than okay with her. She couldn't wait to see their expressions.

Their footsteps neared, echoing down the long marble corridor. When they stopped, nearly tripping over their lolling tongues, she reached deep inside her to the woman she'd always longed to be but didn't think she could embody. It was too late to half-ass it now.

"Welcome home. I hope you're hungry."

"Starving," Ford rumbled as he strode toward her.

Though she hated her momentary weakness, she held up her hand, warding him off. Only for a moment. Until she came clean.

"Wait, please." Kari swallowed hard. "There's something I need to tell you first."

Would they still look at her like they wanted to devour her after she admitted what she'd done the night before?

6

Ford froze a few feet from Kari. His gaze focused on her cleavage. Josh, however, seemed to be paying closer attention to her objection.

He grinned. "Does it have to do with you and Brady sleeping together?"

"Um, yes. So you know about that?" She bit her lip.

"It'd be hard not to. That fucker has been bouncing around all damn day, ever since he told us what happened while we were driving into work," Ford practically growled. "Being productive, whistling in his office for hours at a time and shit. It's pathetic."

Kari didn't agree. It warmed her heart to know that she could make him that happy simply by doing something that made her feel the same way.

"Are you mad?" she asked, afraid to meet the guys' stares.

"Why would we be?" Ford asked as Josh closed the gap between them.

Josh reached out and drew her to the edge of the table so that he could take her fingers in his. He raised them to his lips and kissed her knuckles. He promised, "Of course not, Kari. When it comes to us, you're free to do whatever —or whoever—feels right to you."

She relaxed, breathing deep for the first time since she'd woken up that morning. This was progress. Maybe they could navigate these waters after all. "Okay then. Is it true Brady isn't coming home tonight? Or at least not for a while?"

"Yup. And it serves him right." Ford grinned. "He might have been the appetizer, but now we'll serve you the main meal."

Josh punched him in the shoulder. "Quit that or she'll think you're serious."

Ford paused. "I'm not going to lie. Knowing he had you first made me jealous as fuck...for about three minutes. Until I remembered what it is we're hoping to build here. There's no reason you have to wait for him. He won't be upset if you choose to be with us. But I understand if that's not what you want tonight, or if you tell us to leave you alone entirely, though I'm hoping this incredibly sexy outfit means that's not what you're about to say."

Kari decided to trust them. To trust the process of building whatever the hell this might turn out to be between them. Besides, she'd be lying if she told herself she hadn't been imagining what it would be like in bed with the two of these guys.

"I've never done this before," she admitted.

"What? Fooled around with two guys at once?" Ford asked.

Kari nodded. "I know the three of you have... experimented. I haven't. I don't know if I can handle it. Or if I'll be able to make it good for both of you."

Hell, with Brady, she'd practically just lain there, absorbing the pleasure he'd rained on her. Not exactly a porn-star-worthy performance. Would guys like them— experienced, adventurous—really be turned on by her when it came down to it?

"Let us worry about that." Ford stepped closer.

"If you enjoy yourself, we will too." Josh leaned in and kissed her forehead. "Most of all, we get off on pleasing the woman we're with. Blowing her mind and making her so lost in ecstasy that we're sure we could never be as good for our partner if we were with her on our own."

A shiver raced up her spine, making goose bumps break out on her arms. "That sounds good. I'll have that."

Ford laughed, then grew stern again. "If at any time it doesn't turn out to be as great as you expected or if it's simply too much too soon, say so. Promise me you'll tell us."

"I will. Thank you."

She couldn't stay still a moment longer. They were offering her everything she desired with an easy out should what she thought she wanted turn out to be not what she wanted after all once she tried it. They were perfect. She ached to give them even a fraction of the joy they inspired in her.

Kari leapt toward Ford, who caught her easily. He chuckled again as he spun her around. It was a sound she hadn't heard often enough in the time she'd known him. To be able to change even something so small boosted her confidence.

What if she could make a bigger impact in their lives? If this was what they really craved, she owed it to herself —and to them—to see if it could work.

Okay, that was a little noble. She wanted to fuck them just as much. Desperately.

Kari loved the security of Ford's huge hands cupping her ass, using his grip to pull her fully against his hard cock. She wrapped her legs around him so that she could grind on his length, which pressed to her core as she lowered her lips to his. He wasn't nearly as gentle as Brady had been.

She liked it. Enjoyed surrendering to the part of herself that wanted a forceful man. Even better was knowing Josh was there, and that he'd never let either of them get too carried away. He was her safety net. Her sexy chaperone. And he would make sure that as intense as this exchange was, it was also fun. Flirty.

Josh shuffled up behind her and began to rub her back. "You look so good together. It's making me want you even more. You're going to taste incredible when it's me feasting on you like that."

Kari whimpered and tipped her head back, breaking contact with Ford. He switched his focus to her neck, sucking not-so-gently below her ear, where she was sure he would leave his mark. She didn't care. In fact, she'd be proud to wear it.

All she wanted was to grant Josh his wish. She rested her head on his shoulder, then turned her face toward him. "What are you waiting for?"

His eyes were warm and eager as he studied her. "Are you sure you're ready for this?"

"If you don't kiss me soon, I'm going to call Brady and tell him to get his ass home to do it for you." Kari had no idea where that had come from. They brought out parts of herself she had never realized existed. A needy, sex-kitten side that—now that she'd discovered it—wanted to come out and play more often.

"Nah, I got this." He smiled before lowering his head toward hers. Unfortunately, the awkward angle meant they didn't quite connect.

Ford helped by fisting her hair and lifting her face into the perfect position to accept Josh's kiss. Fuck, that did insane things to her insides. Not to mention how wet it was making her.

Kari's eyes fluttered closed as the sharp tug on her scalp contrasted with the playful contact of Josh's lips. She hadn't forgotten what it was like to kiss him. That night on their catamaran had been magical, and tonight was doubly so. No, truly it was more than that. Like having both Ford and Josh focused on her magnified their effects until it was three times as good as each of them separately. Their impact on her rapture was exponential.

She couldn't get too scientific about it because she was mindless, responding on instinct to Josh's tongue and Ford's teeth raking down her throat. Shamelessly, she squirmed in his hold, rubbing the ache between her legs over the bulge of his erection.

More, she needed so much more.

Ford lifted his head. "Josh, over there."

In sync, they walked toward the gleaming grand piano between the dining table and the living area. She expected them to detour toward the giant sectional sofa once they passed it. They didn't.

"Sit on the bench, facing the piano. It's about time we use this thing for something other than a decoration."

Was Ford serious? Kari looked up at him with wide eyes.

"I figure it'll be the performance of a lifetime." His accompanying grin was wicked.

Kari squirmed in his hold, eager to be beyond the intro of their sensual symphony. Her eyelids seemed to weigh a thousand pounds each. She could hardly open them to take in the scene before her.

Ford lifted her and arranged her so she was splayed on her back, nearly naked, on the cool, glossy surface of the magnificent instrument. The position made it easy for him to place her feet on Josh's shoulders. Ford hooked his fingers in the edge of the tiny lace panel covering her pussy then yanked it aside, giving his partner a perfect view of her soaked folds.

Josh licked his lips, erasing any doubts or insecurities she might have had.

"What are you waiting for?" Ford slapped Josh on the back. "Go down on her. Make her come. Get her good and slick for us."

Josh did as he was told. He held her ankles, one on each side of him, in his tight grasp as he leaned forward and buried his face in her flesh. When he moaned against her already soaking pussy, she shuddered. It wouldn't take much lapping from his skilled tongue to push her over the edge.

He sucked on her clit with light pulses that guaranteed she would shatter the instant he sank his middle finger into her.

In embarrassingly short order, Kari came hard, her eyes rolling back as Josh chased her bucking hips with his mouth to extend her pleasure as long as possible. And when she thought he might stop, he only altered his masterful caresses. Just enough to keep from stimulating her too directly on her sensitized skin.

"You're not getting off that easily," Ford told her.

"Actually...I already did," she said with a smirk and a nervous laugh.

"You will again. And again, and again, before we move on. Josh loves to eat pussy. Especially yours, it seems." Ford strode around the piano until he was near her head. "And I love watching you come."

He planted his palm beside her, crouched, and then sprang, landing on top of the piano with enough force that the vibration rang through the penthouse. All she could do was stare at his rippling abs and try not to drool. When had he shed his clothes?

Kari wasn't sure, but she wished she could lick every exposed inch of his body. She parted her lips.

"Is that what you want?" Ford asked her. "To suck me while Josh eats you?"

She opened her mouth wider in invitation. A shudder wracked her in response to Josh's renewed enthusiasm. He seemed to like that idea. A lot.

Good thing, since Ford was advancing. His knees hit the polished black surface as he tipped forward, planting one fist on the opposite side of her body. His cock hung heavy over her face, nearly within reach.

"See what you do to me?" he said as he stroked his stiff cock. It was huge and hard, straining against his fist as he pumped it.

Kari reached for him. She brushed his hand away and wrapped his shaft in her hand, loving the feel of its heat and heft in her fist. He was even bigger than he'd appeared a moment ago. She purred, imagining what it would feel like when she finally had him where she really wanted him most—fucking her pussy.

She tugged, drawing him closer until she could put his

dick in her mouth. He groaned at the first touch of her tongue on the head of his shaft. Without waiting for him to close the gap, she lunged upward, sheathing him in a single long swoop that nearly made her choke.

Immediately, he withdrew. Not entirely, but enough to keep her calm and in control. Only when she put her hand on his tight ass and pressed did he give her more.

Josh used her distraction to ramp her up again. He toyed with her until she could stand the full contact of his mouth on her pussy once more. As her arousal grew, she sucked Ford harder, hoping her aggression would translate somehow to what Josh was doing to her.

"She wants it," Ford croaked to Josh. "Make her come again."

More than what they did to her body, the way they understood her desires and played off each other to attend to her needs amplified her arousal. Not only did they anticipate what she craved, they gave her that and then some. Their intrinsic awareness turned her on more than even their expert physical prowess.

Josh patted her hip then, as if promising he would deliver. He swirled his tongue around her opening then toward her clit. His fingers found their way back inside her body, introducing several instead of only one this time. He pumped them as he worked her with his mouth.

He spread his fingers apart, making it easy for her to imagine one of the guys sliding his erection deep into her channel, fucking into her while the other paid attention to stimulating her clit.

Shit, it was going to feel so good. Even better than whatever Josh was doing to her now. It was getting harder to concentrate on the specifics when pure bliss took over so much of her awareness. Her thighs trembled as she tried to corral her mounting pleasure.

Ford unwound the lingerie from her so that he could reach down and pinch her nipple, drawing her attention to him. She shifted her gaze without letting him fall from her mouth.

"Don't hold back." He rocked his hips, feeding her every inch of his erection. "Show Josh what a good job he's doing. Come for us. I promise it won't be the last time tonight if that's what you want."

Seriously? Kari was so used to hanging on, making sure to save up her ecstasy until the right moment and will it to be enough. She'd never had a boyfriend who encouraged her to be so...greedy.

She'd be lying if she said she didn't like being spoiled. Who wouldn't?

Josh hummed against her, making her sure he was hungry to taste her desire. That thought alone pushed her over the edge. Kari moaned around Ford's dick and sucked it hard as her body spasmed. She loved the contrast of the unforgiving wood beneath her as she writhed in their warmer, more welcoming, hold.

Rapture exploded around her and triggered an avalanche of moans and praise from the guys.

"Yes, Kari. Yes. You look so damn beautiful." Ford stroked her hair, smiling down at her. "I knew you would. Imagined this moment so many times..."

The thought alone extended her orgasm, making her hug Josh's fingers until they squeezed from her body. She groaned at the loss.

"You want more?" Ford asked.

Kari nodded, the motion bobbing her mouth over his cock a few more times. With a sigh, he withdrew. She tried to reclaim him but he moved off the edge of the piano, dropping gracefully to the floor like a tiger on the hunt.

Then he reached for her, gathering her against his chest. She snuggled into his protective arms, content to lie in them for as long as he'd keep her there.

The intermission of their performance was short-lived.

"Josh, turn around. Straddle the bench, facing sideways." Again, Ford directed the action.

Kari didn't stress about whatever he had in mind. For once, she let someone else be the worrier. The kinky scheme he had devised would be for her benefit. That's all she needed to know. She would be a very willing participant.

"How are you doing?" Josh asked even as he wiped his mouth on his forearm. "Do you feel okay?"

"Amazing." She grinned as she realized the apparent satisfaction in her tone was answer enough. Endorphins were the best painkiller she could imagine for her body, and her mind was fully onboard with their romp.

"Are you sure you want to go further?" He swallowed as he stared at her draped over his partner's muscled arms. "He's not playing around. This is about to get serious."

"It's been serious," Ford corrected. "For longer than just tonight. I've always been serious about us."

"I realize that now." She looked up at him and smiled, laying her palm on his cheek before turning back to Josh to say, "Yes."

Only that single word was required to send them down a path they all knew ended up somewhere very intimate. Josh held his arms up and open. Ford stepped closer and handed her over to his friend.

Kari settled onto his lap, kissing his cheek before burying her face against his neck to breathe deep of the scent of his skin. It reminded her of an ocean breeze or maybe that was just her memory flashing back to the night he'd first kissed her on the water.

He took her hand in his and pressed her fingers over his heart. It pounded in time to her own. Somehow, that made her feel better.

Ford and Josh might be more experienced in this kind of play, but they were every bit as excited as her. With Ford in control, they were free to enjoy the moment. Kari wanted nothing more than to stop thinking entirely and simply react to the attraction arcing between them.

So that's what she did.

7

"Since you're sure you're ready for this, what are we sitting here chatting for?" Ford strode around them like a conductor preparing to take the stage. His fluid grace thrilled Kari as she imagined what it would be like if he was focusing that effort on fucking her instead.

She didn't think she was going to have to wait long to find out.

"Put her here," Ford ordered as he pointed to the empty portion of the bench in front of him, between Josh's splayed thighs.

Josh didn't ask any questions. He did as instructed, settling Kari face down so her chest was pressed to the bench. She gasped as the cool, smooth surface tightened her nipples. Ford took her legs and guided them downward until her toes touched the floor.

Kari peeked up at Josh. She should say something to let him know how much he'd already given her since she hadn't felt this loose and relaxed...well, ever.

"You're really good at that, you know. Thanks," she whispered to him before craning her neck.

He obliged by leaning down to steal a kiss while they were en route to whatever dirty destination Ford had in mind.

"Anytime." Josh winked. "Seriously, you're delicious. I could never get enough of you."

She shivered.

When her feet touched the floor, she wasn't sure she could support herself on her own. But she shouldn't have worried, because neither of them expected her to. Ford grasped her hips and lifted her ass into the air, raising her into a position that made it clear what he had in mind.

Kari braced herself with her hands at chest level, one on either side of the bench. She clung to it as the men stared at her, fully exposed to them.

"Damn," Josh muttered.

"I'm going to fuck her. I can't wait anymore," Ford told Josh, though Kari understood he spelled it out for her benefit as well. He was giving her the chance to object. She didn't.

"Please, don't. Wait, I mean." Kari reached blindly behind her until she snagged his thigh and yanked him closer. Of course, she barely applied any pressure before he was stepping toward her. He kicked the insides of her ankles lightly, urging her to spread herself wider.

When she thought she might tip over, he was there, increasing the grip of his huge hands around her waist and adjusting her so that their pelvises were better aligned.

His cock brushed over her core, making her gasp. Ford ground them together. He couldn't quite seem to tip himself inside given the angles of their bodies.

"Need a hand?" Josh asked with a soft laugh. Was he joking?

If he was, he should have thought better of it, because Ford took him up on his offer. "Actually...yes. Put me inside her."

Those words alone caused an aftershock to wring Kari's channel. She cried out when Josh leaned over her back to grab ahold of Ford's cock and aim it at her opening. When it nudged her there, she moaned and rocked back, trying to embed him.

He took one hand from her waist just long enough to smack her ass. That did nothing to deter her or to stifle her pleasure. Tingles spread from her cheek up her spine. No one had ever done that to her before, but now she understood why some people were into it.

Kari could easily get addicted to the rush of sensations bombarding her now.

Ford's cock began to burrow inside her, coaxing her open with short thrusts that wedged him deeper and deeper. Josh ran his hand along her spine, up to her shoulder. He tangled his hand in her hair and applied pressure until she raised her face toward him. As soon as she did, he was there, seeking entrance to her mouth.

"It looked so good when you were sucking Ford. I want your lips and tongue on me. To know what it's like when you're lost in pleasure and reacting on instinct."

How could she resist that?

Kari licked his shaft, gaining a sense of how different he was from Ford and where he enjoyed her attention most. She nuzzled his balls, surprised when he gasped. If he hadn't had her hair wrapped around his wrist, tethering her to him, she might have jerked away.

"Shhh." Ford petted her flank then, pausing his

advances until she and Josh were settled. "He liked it a little too much, that's all. You're not hurting him."

How could he read her so well? Kari didn't know or care right then. It comforted her to know that they understood and they weren't going to let things go off the rails for any of them.

This time she took Josh in her mouth, sucking lightly on his sac. He sighed, then leaned closer. After she'd taken her time laving his balls until he began to chant her name, she wandered up his shaft, her mouth open and her lips dragging along the engorged shaft.

"You're going to blow his mind, aren't you?" Ford chuckled then.

She was sure as hell going to try. Although it got slightly more difficult when Ford began to distract her once more. The moment she took Josh fully in her mouth, Ford drove forward. The motion pressed Josh against the opening to her throat and embedded Ford in her pussy.

She felt pinned—caught between them, yet surrounded by their strength.

Josh wormed his hand beneath her to palm her breast and Ford mimicked the gesture, except he focused on cupping her pussy. His fingers spread around his cock where it impaled her. Kari stood on her tiptoes and wiggled her ass, trying to get him to move.

"You need me to fuck you?" he asked as he bumped his abdomen against her ass, plunging in a bit deeper.

Kari's eyes rolled back. She couldn't respond except by sucking Josh harder, letting him know exactly how excited she was.

"Do that more," Josh panted. "She likes it."

"I'm going to do better than that." Ford squeezed her

as he withdrew almost entirely then slid into her with a single long stroke.

Kari would have collapsed if he hadn't been supporting her. She realized that even without Ford's hand spiraling closer to her clit, she would have been on the verge of another climax. With it, she didn't stand a chance of lasting.

Not that she really wanted to. Hell, tonight was about reveling in excess.

"She's getting tighter around me," Ford told Josh. "Hugging me, damn. She's making me work for this pussy."

Kari moaned and braced herself as Ford began to ride her faster and harder. That did nothing to reduce her arousal. In fact, every pass of his cock over her engorged flesh brought her one step closer to paradise. She closed her eyes and let the guys take over.

Josh matched Ford's rhythm, slipping in between her lips as Ford fucked her from behind. The massage of Josh's fingers on her breasts added to the full ensemble of sensations they orchestrated for her.

"You're going to come again, aren't you?" Ford asked, though the answer was obvious.

Kari nodded anyway, swirling her tongue around Josh in the process.

Ford rewarded her by strumming her clit with precisely the right amount of pressure to trigger her orgasm. She pulled her head back so she wouldn't risk biting Josh and screamed, surprising herself with the primal sound that burst from her chest.

Ford took mercy on her trembling legs. He slid one hand upward from her waist until it was just below her chest, where it met the bench. He lifted her upright and held her tight against his body—her back to his front—as he kept fucking up into her and letting her ride the waves of her climax.

When she finally opened her eyes and saw Josh staring at them with obvious desire, it rekindled her own arousal. Of course, Ford's fat cock inside her might have had something to do with that too. He shifted, reminding her that he was still buried deep.

"Damn," he whispered in her ear. "That was incredible. *You're* incredible. I can't stay like this or I'm going to lose it."

Josh smiled then. "Don't worry. I've got this." He took his painfully erect cock in hand and stroked it a few times, as if he needed the stimulation. Probably did, since she'd left him hanging.

Kari licked her lips, remembering how he'd tasted and how he'd felt like silk-wrapped steel in her mouth.

"I have other plans," he said to her as he splayed his legs and patted the top of his thigh. "Why don't you come sit on my lap and give Ford a break?"

She was starting to see how having two lovers allowed them to extend her pleasure nearly infinitely. When things got too intense for them, one could back off while the other kept her going. Working together, they ensured she never lost the glow of arousal.

Ford held her as he pulled out, making them both groan. He kissed her temple then promised, "I'll be back. Just need a minute to settle down."

She nodded, then flew to Josh's open arms. He wrapped them around her and did most of the work supporting her weight as she clambered into place. She sensed a shadow of discomfort in her injured leg, but it wasn't about to keep her from enjoying the rest of this night. Pleasure far outweighed her pain. Kneeling on the piano bench, she reached behind her to guide Josh's cock to her drenched pussy.

This was it. She'd had Brady. Then Ford. And now Josh. Finally.

Despite how hard she'd just come, it still felt incredible when he slipped inside. Hot and long, he filled her. Even better, as she instinctively began to ride him, her clit brushed over the muscles he honed in the guys' private gym on the other side of the penthouse. The stimulation was less direct than Ford's fingers had been and gave her time to recover without being too sensitive to enjoy it.

Damn, they knew what they were doing and used every shred of their sinful knowledge to bring her to greater heights. She wasn't about to complain.

In fact, that thought revved her up again. She found her rhythm easily on Josh, aided by his hands around her waist. It felt natural as she began to use his body to create ecstasy they both shared. She couldn't say what made her do it, but she leaned in and put her head on his shoulder as she ground over him. His neck was right there in front of her mouth, her warm breath buffeting his damn skin. And suddenly she had to feel it between her lips and then her teeth.

She sucked and bit the vulnerable spot, and he responded with a roar. Not of pain, but of intense pleasure. His cock jumped within her. Kari couldn't deny that it did something utterly wicked to her to know she could have that kind of impact. Without warning, she shattered, coming on him hard and fast.

"Ford!" Josh groaned, asking for assistance.

"I'm right here. I've got you." Was he talking to Kari or Josh? Maybe both.

Strong hands gripped her from behind and raised her off of Josh's cock. Ford took his place again, hardly giving her a second to mourn the loss of his partner's dick. He didn't give her time to relish her orgasm either, preferring to fuck her through it so that it seemed to keep going forever. By the time it stopped, she was already reaching for the next one.

Kari could get used to that.

She turned into an animal, clawing Josh while trying to thrust backward and take Ford deeper. She was untamed and free and high on rapture. Before she knew what was happening, she was struggling to breathe as another orgasm washed over her.

"My turn," Josh growled at Ford.

Except Ford didn't quit pumping into her. His cock rubbed over her, making her howl for more.

"I'm dying here. I need to be inside her again," Josh practically begged.

Ford leaned down then, blanketing Kari's back. He murmured in her ear, "Do you trust me?"

"Of course," she gasped, trying to catch her breath. Wondering how they were going to ramp things up even further, taking care of them all.

"Josh, put your cock in her," Ford commanded.

"But you're..."

"I didn't say I was going anywhere." He dared his friend to object, frozen as if expecting Kari to do it herself.

She didn't.

"Ford..." Josh groaned.

"Get in here. I'm not stopping now." Ford grunted as

he thrust into her. His strokes had lost some of their precision. His control slipped.

Once she realized holding both of them within her at once was possible, Kari wanted nothing more than that. She opened her mouth and made herself clear. "Yes. That's what I need. Both of you. Together. Please, fuck me."

Josh cursed as he grabbed his shaft and pressed it toward her. He didn't need more encouragement, but the logistics and the newness of the situation meant it took a few tries to line everyone up.

When they had it right, the tip of Josh's cock horned in along Ford's shaft, spreading her impossibly around their cocks.

Josh looked at her as if asking for permission to proceed. Kari was too far gone to be afraid. She nodded, then craned her neck toward him so they could kiss as he squeezed inside her beside Ford.

He thrust into her from below, filling her beyond belief.

"Oh God!" she shouted to no one in particular.

"Too much?" Ford asked.

"Not enough. More. Give me all of you," she told Josh, staring directly into his eyes.

He complied. With a fluid arc of his hips, he embedded himself alongside Ford. All three of them gasped. Kari figured the guys' balls were touching given how deeply they were tucked inside her.

That thought somehow only made her more wanton. She ground down on them, squeezing their cocks together in her channel. She'd never felt so full, as if she might burst and ecstasy would gush out from within her.

Kari's eyes widened and she sucked on Josh's tongue in

time to his advances. It might have been her imagination, but she thought Josh got off on being the bottom of their pile of sweaty, sexy bodies.

It was easier in this position if Ford and Josh stayed still while she kept them together. So she dug her fingers into Josh's shoulders, claiming him as surely as he had her. He got her point and let her sink over him as she swung her ass down and back, gloving both Ford and Josh entirely. Then she rose up on her knees a bit, allowing them to massage parts of her she was sure had never been touched before.

It felt so good she did it again, and again, until she was fucking them both, making Josh pound the bench on either side of her legs. His head was thrown back, his neck exposed as he clenched his jaw.

"Fuck yes. Kari, look what you're doing to him. To us." Ford might have been staying relatively immobile, letting her have her way with him, but he was every bit in control. "He's struggling already, trying not to come inside you and flood your pussy full of his seed."

"Not helping," Josh groaned, his head thrashing.

"How about this? Does this help?" Kari swiveled her hips, bringing their encounter closer to the finale by thrilling them both in a crescendo of bliss.

Josh attempted to say something, but his words were garbled. He took her face in his hands and pulled it toward him, trying again with his lips against her mouth. The only thing she understood was the way his cock felt inside her, right next to Ford's.

Impossible to resist.

She wasn't about to stop kissing him long enough for him to regain his ability to speak either. He trembled beneath her, shuddering as Ford rocked her over him with the power of his own renewed fucking. Just when she thought she might not be able to make her trembling muscles cooperate, Ford took up the slack.

Kari imagined his cock sliding across Josh's within her, driving them all toward ecstasy.

Then Josh groaned. His eyes were open, looking straight into hers. She saw every detail, his pupils dilating and the irises darkening impossibly as he relented. Josh came. His cock twitched inside her, pouring jet after jet of come deep into her pussy, and—presumably—over Ford's hard-on as well.

"Fuck yeah." Ford didn't seem to mind. "I'm about to lose it too."

Kari shuddered, now in a constant state of climax. Her pussy wrung Josh dry.

And when he went limp beneath her, Ford lifted her off of him, keeping her from squashing him against the hard edges of the piano.

He carried her a few feet away, toward the window. She put her palms on the glass and welcomed the coolness as he kept fucking into her from behind.

"Can anyone with a pair of binoculars see us right now?" Kari wondered with a gasp.

"Would it turn you on or make you shy if I say yes?" Ford growled in her hair, against her ear. "Because I love the idea of the whole world watching me claim you. Even if that makes me a barbarian."

Josh echoed him with a happy moan. She expected him to deny it, but he didn't.

Being possessed by them did something to Kari. It unlocked something inside her she hadn't realized she'd stuffed into a box—no, a cage—after her incident with

Marty. Sometimes it was okay to give yourself up. To become someone else's if they were yours too.

Rather than object, or go cold, Kari embraced the moment. *Let them watch! See me fly!*

She stared out at the twinkling lights of the city as Ford twitched within her. "You're strangling my dick. You want me to keep going, don't you?"

"Yes, please." Kari would die if he didn't start moving again.

He pulled nearly all the way out, then slammed back inside. The sparks he sent through her made her spine arch, which drove Ford deeper.

"Damn," he hissed before wrapping his hands around her waist and anchoring her there, impaled fully on his shaft. "You're so soft and wet and hot as fuck."

Kari rocked against him, then forward, granting them both the barest bit of relief as the head of his cock rubbed against sensitive places deep within her body.

"Shhh. I'm going to give you what you need," Ford said. "I'm going to come inside you. And I want you with me."

"I don't know if I can anymore." She let her forehead rest on the glass. Was she still coming from the last time or had her body simply began to hum like a tuning fork they'd struck repeatedly? It had gotten hard to tell.

"You will. One more time." It wasn't an order, it was a promise. "You're so sexy, and so responsive. You were made to be ours. Or maybe we were made to be yours. All three of us. You can handle our desires. This."

He rocked his hips and she moaned, wanting more even now.

"Exactly," he murmured in her ear as he began to fuck

her again. "You're everything we've dreamed of. Sweet. Sexy. And hungry as hell."

Kari felt herself tightening at Ford's dirty talk. He was right. This was going to happen again and soon. It was too intense, too incredible to be a slow-burn situation. No, this was going to be the Fourth of July, condensed into thirty seconds of the most epic grand finale she could imagine.

Ford laughed. He actually laughed. Right there in the middle of the most intense experience of her life. It was the sort of triumphant, glorious laughter that made her sure he'd been waiting forever for this moment himself.

"You're incredible, Kari," he whispered before his hand snaked around her hip. His fingers roved over her mound, until he forked them on either side of his shaft.

Kari kept still as he manipulated her, unable to relax until she'd let him scratch the itch she hadn't even known she'd had before. When his thumb pressed over her clit then drew repetitive circles around it, she knew their time was limited.

"See?" he hissed as he pumped inside her faster, harder. "Trust me, Kari. I know what we need. And right now, I need you to fall apart with me."

A tidal wave of pleasure crashed over her. She screamed and her entire body clenched. Every muscle she had flexed and held for the longest moment. Then they spasmed, wringing endless pleasure from Ford's cock while delivering as much as she received in return.

Ford couldn't resist her euphoria. Apparently, neither could Josh. He cheered them on as Ford became frantic, fucking into her with erratic strokes.

He shot every drop of his own release into her, where it mingled with Josh's and Kari's own slickness. She kept moving involuntarily, grinding on him until her bones began to melt and she resembled a wet noodle more than the sex goddess she'd embodied minutes earlier.

She went limp, collapsing in Ford's arms. He caught her to his heaving chest, keeping her steady when she couldn't. He stayed there, his breath heaving, reminding her of a racehorse that had just shattered a world record until he slipped from her body.

"I'll take her," Josh said quietly from beside them right before his hands wrapped around her ribs and she felt herself being lifted into his arms.

Her eyes were already drifting closed. She let herself float through a cloud of natural and manmade chemicals, not to mention emotions, as the last pulses of her orgasm swept through her.

"Let's go upstairs," Ford told Josh, who nodded then followed with her, a step behind. He smiled down at her when she peeked up at him while he climbed the stairs to their personal space. Ford turned toward the bedroom they'd lent her.

"Are we invited to stay the night?" Josh asked as Ford watched him set her gently onto the bed.

"I'll be pissed if you don't," she responded without thinking. "Unless you're good. You know, now that we…"

Josh was already snuggling up beside her. "This is new, so I won't let what you're saying bug me. You don't know how bad I need all of you yet. But I'm going show you."

Ford didn't say anything. Neither did he disagree. He climbed in the side of the bed opposite from Josh and stretched out beside her. He kissed her forehead and said, "Thank you. This was the best night of my life."

"And hopefully not as good as others to come," Kari said as she smiled dreamily up at him. None of them mentioned it, but she was wondering what it would be like if Brady had been there. And how he would feel when he discovered he'd been the one left out this time. It was almost worse than having sex with just one of them when she fucked two.

Next time she'd have to rectify that mistake.

Kari was still smiling as she cuddled, sandwiched between two of the three hottest men in her life. Despite her exhaustion, she couldn't stop staring at them in awe as they drifted off, exhausted.

8

Kari couldn't sleep.

Not because she wasn't worn out from the night before, but because she was amped up. Honestly, she also couldn't wait to see Brady and make sure things were still okay between them.

Ford and Josh had seemed certain he wouldn't give a shit that they'd indulged without him. In some weird way, that stung. After all, she'd be devastated if they left her out. Maybe they weren't as invested as she was. Could it be this was simply a physical affair for them?

They certainly hadn't talked about the two big F's— their feelings or the future. Along with fucking, she figured those completed the trifecta of the perfect relationship. One cornerstone was taken care of. The previous two nights had blown her mind.

But the rest?

It was killing her to wonder about what was to come and if she'd left herself open to the kind of pain that hurt far worse than being hit by a taxi. So instead of lying in bed, she snuck away from the heat and comfort of Josh and Ford's tangled limbs.

Kari decided to work on a fourth, very important, F. Food.

She was part of the way through making eggs Benedict with hollandaise sauce when a noise to her left startled her. Brady shuffled through the hallway opening into the main living area of the penthouse. His hair was smooshed flat to his head and the shadow under his eyes rivaled her own. "Holy shit. Are you just now getting home?"

He nodded, his face set in a grim line.

Kari wiped her hands on the far-too-large apron with *I'm grilling a witness* embroidered on it and jogged over to him. "Is everything okay?"

"Not really." He scrubbed his hands over his stubbled face. "I'm sorry, Kari. I've tried everything and, in my professional opinion, we don't have enough yet to put Marty away for this. It's circumstantial at best."

"It was him." She put her hands on her hips, trying not to shake. If they couldn't pin her attack on that bastard, he'd be out there, waiting for another opening to hurt her again. He wasn't going to give up. She remembered how he'd tailed her, and the feel of his hand on her breastbone as he'd propelled her into the street.

Suddenly, the smell of her burning food sickened her.

"I know, honey." Brady reached out and gathered her to his chest as if he needed reassurance that she was okay as much as she did. "We're going to have to wait him out for now, though."

The disappointment in his tone twanged something inside her. Was he bummed that it could take a while? An insecurity left over from the days after Marty had first attacked her and made her feel less-than. She had no intention of imposing or assuming that because they'd slept together, their actions meant something more to him. Getting her hopes up then finding out she was wrong would be even more humiliating than the outright cruelty she'd faced in the past. "How long are you really going to want me crashing your place? Do all your flings move in until you get bored of them?"

"*Fling*?" Brady practically growled. His face went slack. He dropped his arms and took a massive step away. "Is that what this is to you?"

She felt the distance he'd slammed between them in every molecule of her being. She reeled, realizing how much his rejection could damage her. What if she forgot how to stand on her own? A day or two here, with them, and she'd already gotten used to leaning on them.

Kari winced. If Brady wasn't going to reassure her, she sure as hell wasn't going to stick her neck out first and admit that she was terrified her feelings for him—*them*— meant this was a lot more than a casual affair. She had no right to assume they would sign up for more than a few fucks.

Sure, they treated her with respect and pampered her. That didn't mean that they were in it for more than sex. She'd already used such poor judgment once, letting her guard down around Marty. Look how that had turned out. Maybe she was making a huge mistake again.

Maybe it was best to keep that space wedged between them, insulating her from the effects of being close to him, so she could think clearly about where they were headed before she got in too deep to save herself.

When she didn't say anything, Brady cursed. He jammed his hands in his hair and spun toward the windows, acting a lot more like Ford than himself. "Damn it, Kari. I'm too tired to do this right now."

Brady's exhaustion might have had something to do with how he lashed out. Or maybe he was too weary to hide his true feelings from her in that moment.

Either way, she had to put some distance between them. Find her footing on her own again. Because this could end at any moment and she couldn't get too attached to them or it would really fuck her up when they left her alone.

Kari had lived through trauma once. Somehow, she thought this might be even more painful. Marty hadn't ever cared for her or even pretended to. His actions had been a violation of her body. This involved more than her flesh.

The injuries she sustained from reckless involvement could go even deeper than pure abuse.

"I've got to go. Enjoy breakfast. It looks like you could use it." Kari meant that sincerely, not as some sarcastic barb. The way Brady recoiled, she wasn't sure he understood that. So she whipped the apron over her head, balled it up, and put it on the counter before she could make even more of a mess of things than she already had.

"Kari, wait." Brady reached for her. She dodged. If he touched her, he would persuade her to ignore her better sense and she wasn't about to do that again.

No, she had to leave.

Maybe later, when everyone had calmed down and was thinking rationally, they could talk things through. Right then, she had to escape.

Kari snagged her purse off the counter, glad she'd brought it down to get the cell phone charger out of it earlier, then marched for the front entryway. She paused only long enough to slip on her shoes.

"At least let me take you home..." Brady said quietly from the end of the hall. It was far enough away that she could drag in a few shaky breaths despite the crushing pressure in her chest.

"You don't look like you're in any shape to drive. Did you sleep at all? Eat anything?" Kari's shoulders slumped. She should have thought to send him food at least. If she hadn't been busy fucking his best friends, maybe she would have. She was losing sight of important things when she got carried away with them.

Brady didn't respond to her questions, which was answer enough. He tried one more time to sway her, though. "Bronson..."

"Probably waited all night for you and barely crawled into bed himself." Kari reached for the door. She opened it, then promised, "I'll have the front desk downstairs call me a cab and wait inside until the security guard can escort me to the car."

"Oh. Yeah, okay." Brady blinked a few times, as if he couldn't have thought of the suggestion himself. He swayed on his feet, obviously relieved, if about to drop.

"This isn't healthy," she said mostly to herself. Brady's flinch made her sure he'd heard her, though. Kari didn't want to hurt them anymore than she wanted to suffer herself.

Shaking her head she muttered, "Goodbye," then walked out the door.

She impressed herself with her calm, steady tone as she made her request of the staff member manning the front desk then waited for the cab. If she sobbed the entire ride home, well, no one other than the poor driver she tipped generously had to know that.

Confused, she couldn't decide if she'd done what was best for them all despite how it shredded her insides or if she'd fucked things up entirely.

9

Marty hated that bitch.

Not only had she acted like she was too good for him when they'd worked together, she'd gotten him fired. Sure, the triple fuckers had said it was because of the shit that went down with Cooper, but he knew the truth. It was really because he'd dared to take what they wanted.

To top it all off, it seemed like now they were getting Kari's pussy after all. Whatever. It wasn't like he was obsessed with her or how good she'd felt when he'd had her at the company Christmas party. She clearly was slut enough to take care of three guys, what was one more?

Especially if he got some more of those pills. His dealer was right—they made it a lot easier to get her to finally look at him and want him back. Although after that one time, she'd gone right back to treating him like he was some kind of monster. Even though she knew he could get her off just fine.

Maybe he'd have to show her again. Remind her that

she'd liked it no matter what she'd pretended the next day.

This time he wouldn't be so nice about it. Not only had he lost his job, but it seemed like the experience working there—which should have made him a hot commodity at other law firms in the city—couldn't even get him an entry-level interview elsewhere.

Which meant that his old bosses had blacklisted him.

Marty was going to sue the shit out of them.

After he got some more personal revenge.

It seemed like Kari hadn't only recovered from her run in with that cab—she'd moved in with the triple fuckers after a much shorter than anticipated hospital stay.

Marty was positive she hadn't come home yet, because he'd sat in the diner across from her apartment for hours after he'd sent her tumbling into the street. He hadn't intended to push her, at first. Once he had, he kind of liked the rush it gave him.

Finally, something he was in control of.

Even better would be if she accepted the giant bouquet of flowers he'd bought her to say sorry, even if he didn't really mean it. He figured it was a good way to get inside.

Except she hadn't been there to let him in.

Eventually, he'd crept closer. Across the street and up the fire escape perched outside her apartment. It had taken him half the night to work up the courage to force her window open and climb through it so he could leave his surprise for her. The flowers had gotten banged up in his trip, but he'd set them out anyway. It was the thought that counted.

Then, curious, he'd crept through her space, learning more about the things she liked and what she surrounded herself with. Maybe he could win her over after all if he knew more about that.

While he was there, he couldn't help but peek into her dresser until he stumbled across her underwear drawer. He ran his hands through the pretty things inside and felt himself getting hard.

It was only fair that he use Kari's panties to get himself off since she was constantly leaving him in this state. Turning him on without giving him any relief.

Marty shoved a lacy pair down his pants. He wrapped his hand in them, then started to jerk. It didn't take long before he was crumpling the sticky mess he'd made of them into a ball. He was stuffing them in his pocket when a noise caught his attention.

Was that the door? Shit!

Someone was here.

Marty bolted, the scrap of fabric falling from his fingers, instantly forgotten.

He climbed out the window and onto the fire escape. Thankfully, Kari only lived on the second floor, which made it pretty easy to get in and out. You couldn't be in his profession and not have picked up a trick or two.

Maybe he should switch to being a defense attorney. Sometimes people didn't understand the situation and how stuff could get out of hand. Circumstances pushed you to do these things. He'd tried to play nice with Kari, and look where it had gotten him.

Now he was being forced to go to lengths he never would have thought of before. And it was all her fault. Hers, Ford's, Brady's, and Josh's. They were all to blame for this mess.

Cooper and his fuck buddies too.

They were all going to pay for what they'd done to

him. How they'd shunned him and destroyed his career. They would see that they had screwed up royally.

Marty should run. He should climb down the ladder and disappear, but he couldn't resist watching for a moment to see how Kari would react to his surprise.

Maybe she would come to her senses and beg him to stay.

It was the last chance he was going to give her to see things his way.

10

I t took every last bit of strength Kari had to unlock her door and push it open. It wasn't as heavy as the reinforced one at the entrance to Ford, Brady, and Josh's place, but she'd always felt secure here.

When she trod inside far enough to see her living room, she froze. Rose petals were scattered all over. On the furniture, the floor, and even the walls.

How had the guys managed to do that so fast? Was it an apology? Had Brady wanted to prove she was wrong about the nature of their relationship?

Kari's heart flip-flopped in her chest. Could she have gotten it mixed up? Did her knee-jerk reaction have more to do with her own anxieties than reality?

She picked up one of the petals and let it fall through her fingers. A vase caught her eye. That's when she noticed the bouquet inside, and the fact that several of the flowers were crushed or broken. Blood-red petals around her took on a sinister vibe when she realized they had been brutally severed from the ruined stems scattered nearby.

Something wasn't right.

Kari took her phone from her purse and unlocked it. But who should she call?

Ford? No.

The police? That seemed sort of extreme. She had a flash of herself trying to explain her weird instinct. "Yes, someone came into my apartment and left me kind of shitty flowers after the whole world saw me get hit by a car. No, I'm not sure they're not a get-well-soon present from my landlord or my neighbor who has my spare key."

They'd think she was nuts.

So she called Andi.

"Good morning, Kari!" Andi was entirely too happy. It was jarring considering the panic bubbling up within Kari right then.

"Hey." Her voice trembled. "This is kind of crazy..."

"Are you okay?" Andi asked, her entire tone changing as she caught on to Kari's discomfort.

In the background, Reed immediately started barking questions. "Who is that? Kari? Is something wrong?"

Shit. Shit. Shit.

Was it? Kari still couldn't tell. She inched forward and peeked around, noticing her photo albums were out of order on a nearby shelf, and she could swear she had left her slippers a few feet closer to the couch.

"I think so. Maybe? It's just...someone's been in my apartment," Kari whispered, though she couldn't say why. "Would you stay on the phone with me for a second? I'm kind of rattled."

"What makes you think someone was in there?" Andi wondered. "After yesterday, I don't blame you for being afraid. Why don't you turn around and wait for one of us to get there? We'll check it out with you. I'm getting dressed now. Reed is already putting his shoes on."

"I don't think that's necessary. Don't laugh, all right?" Kari was starting to feel silly about panicking. "Whoever it was left flowers. Lots of them. Some of them seem sort of ratty or something. Like they're cheap or have seen better days."

She trailed off, afraid of sounding like a snob. It was one of those things she could sense but couldn't quite put into words.

"You think they're from your guys?" Andi wondered. "Sounds like something they'd do to impress you. But I'm a little confused. I thought you were staying at their place for a while."

"I really don't see how it could have been them." She thought about it some more.

Sure, piles of money could make the seemingly impossible happen sometimes. But arranging something like this in the scant time it had taken for her to catch a cab and cross town... If someone had been in a hell of a hurry, that might explain the damage. Already rattled from her confrontation, she struggled to think straight. Nothing made sense anymore so she confided in Andi. "I just left there. I got in a...*thing*...with Brady."

"Your first fight? Oh, that's cute!" Andi was trying to cheer Kari up. It wasn't working. Cold sweat slipped down her spine. If she had another panic attack, what would her new friend think? "Then I definitely wouldn't put it past him to send flowers to make it up to you. They have enough money to make it happen, even that fast."

Andi confirmed what she'd already been thinking, which meant Kari was probably overreacting.

"You're probably right." She willed herself to relax.

Kari took a deep breath, then another, before releasing a super-awkward, nervous laugh. "I'm sorry I bugged you this early."

"It's no problem. Are you sure you're okay?" Andi asked. "I can pick up some donuts and come over so we can commiserate over how dumb guys can be and why you're absolutely right about whatever it was you were arguing over."

Kari began to reassure her friend that was unnecessary. Except right then the loose floorboard in her bedroom squeaked like it did every time she stepped on it while opening her window. She jumped a mile high. "Who's there?"

"Oh my God!" Andi shouted on her end of the phone. "Reed, call the police. Now!"

Kari was frozen, unable to move her feet or make a single sound other than the rasp of her hyperventilation.

Then Andi was screaming in her ear. "What's happening?"

Through the doorway, she saw the curtain flapping, too strongly to be disturbed by a breeze. No, someone was climbing out of her apartment. Kari rushed around the corner, her head whipping from side to side as she took in the empty bedroom. Was that her underwear on the ground? Why was it wet?

"There's someone on my fire escape. He was watching me. I think he was... Oh God, I'm going to be sick." Kari groaned, still stuck in place.

"Get the hell out of there!" Andi shrieked. "Run!"

Kari should have thought of that herself. She was overwhelmed.

Terrified. Disgusted. Paralyzed.

She shook herself out of it and pivoted, sprinting for

her door. When she crashed into someone in the hallway, she screamed and thrashed.

"Holy shit!" the person said as they tumbled to the ground together, her phone skittering out of her hand.

"Kari, is that you?" her next-door neighbor, Max Green, asked from where he'd landed fully on top of her. It took her a second, and a few jabs of her knee at him —*sorry, Max*—to realize that he wasn't some creeper haunting her.

Kari nearly passed out from relief. She went limp. Couldn't speak. So instead she pointed to her phone where Andi's frantic screams were coming through, garbled but audible despite the distance.

Max lunged for it, then listened. "Hey, this is Max Green. I'm Kari's neighbor. I have her. She's safe. When will the cops be here?"

She could have lost it completely then. Instead, she was filled with rage.

Not only had her body been violated, but now her home had been too. Kari was sure of exactly who that had been outside her window and whose DNA was smeared all over her panties on the floor inside.

"Shit!" Kari scrambled to her feet. "I have to get those."

"What? Where the hell are you going?" Max lunged, trying to grab her. She dodged and busted through the door of her apartment. Not her smartest move ever, but she was willing to risk it to prove—irrefutably—that Marty was the person terrorizing her.

Sure enough, as she rounded the corner, that monster was sneaking back inside to clean up after himself.

Fuck no! Kari raced past him and threw herself on top of the used underwear, huddling over them as he came closer.

"Jesus Christ!" Max roared. "She ran back inside and there's some dude in there with her. We need help. Now! Send more cops. Send the building security. Send anyone!"

Marty halted his advance, no more than a few feet away. As she looked up, she realized he had a heavy stoneware flowerpot in his hands, which were raised high. Kari wrapped her arms over her head, though it would hardly be enough protection to prevent her mini-herb garden from doing what that taxi hadn't.

Max came to the door with a snarl. "Get the fuck out of here before you make this worse for yourself, you creepy bastard! Do this and your life is over, too."

Marty looked at Max, then at Kari—protecting the evidence she desperately needed to make him pay. He took one more step toward her before Max charged.

Faced with such bravery, Marty changed his mind. He dropped the pot with an ominous crash. Shards of pottery accompanied the sound, making it seem like an IED had gone off mere feet from Kari's face.

He fled like the coward he was, leaving her and Max staring in shock.

Kari couldn't help it then. She burst into tears.

The last thought she had before the world erupted into a chaos of sirens and Max's relentless questions was: *I wish Ford, Brady, and Josh were here with me.*

11

Brady pounded his fist on his leg. "Fuck. This is all my fault. I didn't handle things right."

"You were tired and pissed. Frustrated. Hell, even scared. You can't keep blaming yourself every time something goes wrong. We're still figuring things out. We'll get it right even if it takes a couple tries." Josh talked Brady down as Ford concentrated on driving.

He navigated his personal sedan through the city streets at a speed that might require their legal skills if he got caught by the cops. Thankfully, the car was both elegant and fast as fuck.

As much as Ford understood the perfect storm that had brewed between Kari and Brady, he also had a crazy sense of dread and urgency spurring him to fix it as soon as possible.

Brady had woken him and Josh with a shouted stream of curses the likes of which Ford had never heard from his usually rational friend before. When they'd rushed into the kitchen and found him about to yank his hair out, they'd pried out a half-assed explanation of what had gone down.

They hadn't even waited long enough to rouse Bronson before chasing after Kari.

They weren't going to lose her over some bullshit misunderstanding.

She should be with them. In their house—protected, cherished.

Ford realized part of why she'd left had to do with the emotions they were stirring up as their relationship evolved. It was too early to admit what he suspected...that it was love. The real thing. He was constantly stopping himself from thinking it or, God forbid, saying it out loud and spooking her. Worse, he wondered now if hiding his feelings entirely could have been even more dangerous than revealing them too soon.

There had to be some middle ground. It sounded like she didn't understand exactly how committed they were to the bonds they were building and why they were being so damn cautious.

With other women they'd dated—okay, fucked—it hadn't been like this.

Of course, Kari didn't know that. But he planned to enlighten her. Then take her home, hopefully for good.

It was insane how *wrong* it had felt to wake up and realize she was missing. From the bed they'd shared the night before, from their house, and from his life.

His guts had knotted so tight he couldn't even sneak a bite of that incredible meal she'd left cooling on the counter. Hopefully they could hash things out and have her back in time for some make-up brunch they'd use as fuel for another evening like the previous one.

How could she have doubted what they had after that?

Ford knew he'd been convinced the moment she had taken both him and Josh at once, linking them within her, that she was exactly what they needed to be happy. Finally and forever.

Shit, there he went getting ahead of himself again.

Ford smacked the steering wheel when he encountered yet another red light. "Fuck. Come on. Can't we catch a break?"

Josh spoke calmly from the backseat. "Look, I'm as worried as you two, but we can't go rushing up to her door like this. You have to keep it together and show her that we're not psychotic, obsessed, and irrational like Marty. We're logical and patient."

"Speak for your damn self," Ford growled. Right then he had more in common with a cornered feral animal than the kind of man Josh was trying to make him out to be. Fear and doubt nagged him. He didn't like Kari being on her own. Not now. Not when Marty was out there and growing more dangerous by the day.

"I'm being serious," Josh insisted, using the steely tone he usually reserved for the courtroom. When he got down to business, all hints of his affable self disappeared. The playful kid-at-heart was nowhere to be seen. "You two aren't in this on your own. What you do, and how you react, also impacts my chance at happiness. Don't fuck this up for me. For us all."

Brady groaned. "I said I'm sorry."

"Don't be. Let's just make this right, okay?" Josh bumped his fist into Brady's shoulder with a confidence Ford didn't share. What if they couldn't?

The light turned green. He mashed the pedal to the floor.

And that's when his phone started ringing.

He ignored it.

Until it rang again.

Ford took it out of his pocket and tossed it to Josh, who answered for him.

"Hello?" Josh waited, then said, "Hey, Reed. Ford's driving, what do you need?"

Another few seconds passed.

"Yes, we're almost at her place now."

That put Ford on high alert. Everything about Kari did. He tried to calm himself and concentrate on the road, but it was hard not to flashback to the moment they'd found out Kari had been attacked the other day. Was he being overprotective or was there a reason for the foreboding that shot icy tendrils down his spine?

"No, she didn't call us. No, neither did the cops. What the fuck is going on, Reed?" Josh raised his voice.

Ford didn't give a fuck how many tickets he racked up. He accelerated, practically taking out a light post when he hugged the corner.

"Son of a bitch!" Josh shouted. "I'm going to kill him, I swear."

"Josh, what the fuck?" Ford glared in the rearview at his friend.

"Marty. He was in her apartment."

Brady shuddered. He went white as the crisp shirts he wore to court. "He got her. Because of me. Because I let her go…"

"Is she okay?" Ford roared.

"We're about to find out." Josh hung up on Reed, then flew out of the car the moment Ford screeched to a stop at the curb in front of her building.

It was a race to see who got to her first, all three of them pounding up the stairs, not even bothering to wait for the elevator. Who could be still for the eternity that would take?

They slammed through the fireproof door onto her floor, only to come face to face with a dude none of them had seen before. Ford snarled, "Get out of my way."

"I don't think so, asshole." The guy crossed his arms and spread his legs.

Punches might have been thrown if Kari hadn't peeked over his shoulder and said, "Ford? Is that you?"

"Yes, I'm here. *We're* here." He rushed the guy, who stepped aside as Kari tried to sprint past him at the same time.

"Oh, thank God." Kari threw herself into their arms. Josh ended up with the most direct grasp on her, his arms winding around her and clutching her to his chest. Ford stood nearby, running his hands through her hair and down her arm to reassure himself that she was alive and relatively unharmed.

When she began to sob, it wrecked him.

Through not nearly as much as it did Brady, if the look on his friend's face was any indication. Ford demanded, "Get over here, Brady."

The guy shook his head, hovering but not joining their embrace.

Kari sniffled, then looked up at him, her lower lip wobbling. "Please. I need you. I'm sorry."

"*You're* sorry? For what?" He hurried to her then, smothering her between himself, Josh, and Ford.

"I don't know. I can't think right now. I just...don't want to fight." She leaned her head back against his chest and closed her eyes, relaxing in front of their eyes.

"What the fuck happened?" Ford asked. "Where's Marty?"

Kari trembled. "He ran. Max chased him out."

Ford had forgotten all about the man observing them with a keen gaze. Let him stare—who cared?

Unless that was jealousy in the guy's expression.

Untangling himself, Ford stuck out his hand and introduced himself. If he squeezed Max's hand tighter than he would have otherwise, he figured that was understandable guy code.

"I'm Max. Her neighbor." The guy grinned.

Under other circumstances, Ford thought he might like Max. At the very least, he appreciated him coming to Kari's aid. "Thank you."

"It was no big deal." Max shrugged. "It all happened so fast, I reacted on instinct. When she ran back in there with him..."

"You *what*?" Ford rounded on Kari. "Are you insane?"

She laughed at that, which oddly made him feel better. "Maybe a little. But no, I was protecting the evidence."

"What do you mean?" Brady stepped up then, lawyer mode fully engaged.

"I don't want to go in there, okay?" She hugged Josh tighter. "You can, though. In my bedroom. On the floor..."

Ford dashed inside, his phone in his hand. When he saw her underwear on the ground, clearly soiled, he wanted to smash his fist into the mirror. Break things, since Marty wasn't there to hit instead.

Brady said calmly from behind him, "Don't. Don't touch anything. Preserve the scene."

Sirens blared while red and blue lights washed over the windows. They would soon have company. Lots and lots of it.

Ford nodded. He unlocked his phone and snapped as

many photographs as he could in the minute or two it took for cops to swarm Kari's apartment. He hated to admit it, but everything that had happened might have been for the best if it meant they could prove definitively that Marty had been the intruder in her apartment.

Their case against him just got a hell of a lot stronger.

He paced the hallway while detectives interviewed Kari. Josh took over as her watchdog and official representation while he and Brady came to an unspoken understanding. Until they could send Marty away, they weren't letting Kari out of their sight again for a single moment, whether she liked it or not.

It was a good sign that she was still clutching Josh's hand when they left the apartment. Kari seemed smaller than usual, defeated. Lost.

Brady groaned. "Kari..."

She shook her head. "I can't right now. I don't have anything left in me."

"Come home with us," Ford said as gently as he could manage. "You know there's plenty of space. You're welcome to as much of it as you need. No one will bother you or pressure you to talk until you're ready. Just come. And *stay*. Where you'll be safe."

Josh squeezed her fingers. "If it's too much, we'll call Andi, Reed, Simon, and Cooper to come get you, okay? It's not smart for you to be alone until this is...resolved."

If Ford hadn't been staring at her, he might not have noticed her muted grimace. Whether she wanted to admit it or not, she didn't like the idea of spending the time elsewhere any more than they did. Thank God.

Still, she didn't agree until Brady stepped forward, took her hand from Josh, kissed her knuckles, and murmured, "Please."

Then she nodded and followed them to their car without another word.

She tucked against Josh's side and rested her head on his chest for the entire ride home. Whether she was asleep or simply mentally burnt out, Ford didn't know. He drove a lot more carefully on the return journey to their penthouse, unwilling to risk anything happening to her.

He wouldn't be able to handle it if it did again.

12

If Kari had to take another bite of the delicious meal the guys had summoned from a fancy-ass restaurant that didn't offer takeout for mere commoners and pretend like everything was fine, she was going to scream.

She had no idea where to go from here. They were stuck.

At first, she'd been glad they hadn't pressured her to talk about what had happened back at her apartment or —almost worse—the argument with Brady that had spurred her to flee the sanctuary of their home in the first place.

The rest of the day had passed as she curled up on the couch, resting and recovering while reading a book. The guys had pretty much done the same, collecting themselves. At least one of them had hung out with her at all times, though they never intruded on her quiet contemplation.

Their issues had fed off the awkward silence and were hanging there in the air between them, preventing them from moving forward. Easier than hashing things out?

Sure. But it wasn't like them to avoid difficult topics. Leaving their problems unresolved only increased her anxiety until she couldn't handle it any longer.

"Guys?" Kari balled her linen napkin in her hands, then looked from man to man to man. "What the hell is going on here?"

"What? We're sharing a peaceful dinner." Josh raised his glass. "Ignoring anything that could get us into too much trouble. Isn't that what you wanted?"

"Not exactly." Kari sighed, setting her fork and napkin on her plate, then pushing it away from her. She'd rather be wrapped so tightly in them that she couldn't spare a single brain cell to think about what had happened—and worse things that could have happened—that morning.

Jumping into bed before discussing their issues would only lead to more drama in the morning. So she put on her big girl panties and prepared to make herself uncomfortable. Vulnerable in a way that was far more dangerous than the physical danger she'd survived back at her apartment.

"After you quit your job at the firm and then the things you said to me earlier..." Brady swallowed hard, although he hadn't eaten much either. "I get it. We get it. We've been taking things too fast. Giving you the wrong impression."

"I shouldn't have reacted like that. I guess I got nervous and then we accidentally mashed each other's buttons. That was unfair of me," she admitted. "I don't know what I want and that's making me crazy."

"I think you do." Ford stared at her. "And I think that's why you keep running. You're afraid you're going to be disappointed if we're not after the same things."

More like crushed, she thought.

"We are, though." Josh leaned forward. "I swear we are."

"How do you know that?" She winced. "You don't know what's in my mind...or my heart. We never stopped to talk about it."

"Well, we are now." Ford kept eating like nothing was wrong. Maybe he was right and everything was fine. As much as she hated it, she needed that reassurance. "As long as you're ready to hear what we have to say."

She nodded. "I am. I think. No, really. I am."

Kari took a deep if shaky breath. They already had the power to rip her to pieces. Admitting it wouldn't change that, so why not?

"It's important to us that you know we want more than a physical relationship," Brady said. Ford and Josh nodded. "It wasn't our intention to make you think all we had in mind was sex. It's not easy to resist touching you when we're sharing such close quarters. Still, that's no excuse. We'll do better at communicating our feelings, which run deep."

"We kept quiet so we wouldn't scare you away. But it seems like we did anyway," Josh added. "We can wait to fool around more if that's what it takes to show you we intend to make this work for the long haul. You're different from any other woman we've been with and we'll do whatever you need to ensure you're happy in a long-term, exclusive relationship with us. Especially after this morning..."

Ford finally dropped his fork as if he couldn't stomach another morsel after the reminder of what had happened and how much worse it could have been. Funny, discussing dozens of similar cases in the office had never had that effect on him. Could it be true? Were they equally as invested as she was?

A spark of hope flared inside her.

Kari couldn't blame the guys for reacting like they had. Neither did she want this distance to fester between them and screw things up even more. She wouldn't give Marty that much influence over their relationship. He'd ruined enough of her life already.

Before she could second-guess her decision, Kari nudged her chair backward. Instead of rising from the table and walking away to sulk in her room alone, as the guys seemed to expect of her, she stood and began to get undressed.

"Uh, Kari?" Brady asked. "What're you doing?"

Maybe they thought she'd gone nuts after her most recent trauma. Hell, maybe she had.

Because she grabbed the bottom hem of her T-shirt then whipped it off, tossing it over Ford's head to the floor behind him. Next, she unbuttoned her jeans and began to walk them down her hips, revealing the soft pink panties she'd chosen from the stash the guys had arranged to appear in her suite that morning.

They might have been simple, but they were soft and made a statement in their own way.

Very girl-next-door-gone-rogue, which was exactly how she felt right then.

"Kari?" Ford asked more sternly when she didn't respond to Brady. Rather than trying to dissuade her, he took his arm and swiped the dishes from in front of him with one lightning fast motion. The resulting clatter should have made her cringe. Instead, it triggered her grin.

"That's right. You should have me for dessert."

She shrieked with glee when he lunged over the table, wrapped his arm around her waist and hauled her right across the slick surface onto his lap.

Kari paused only long enough to make eye contact with each of her men. "It's the same for me. I don't want to go slower with you. I want to be all in. Let's be honest, I've already been for a while now or I wouldn't have been willing to push so many boundaries, give up my career, or trust you in the darkest times of my life."

"In that case, let's get rid of these." Ford helped her as she squirmed and kicked her jeans off her legs. They flopped over Josh's head and shoulders.

"Wait. Not that I don't love spontaneity, but...we have a perfectly comfortable bed upstairs. Why don't we use it?" Brady wondered. Something in his tone forced Kari to pause. He was speaking in code to his best friends, she was sure of it.

"The one in the special room?" Ford asked, confirming her suspicions.

Josh shook her pants off his head like a dog emerging from a lake, and grinned. "It's time we used it, don't you think?"

"Absolutely." Ford scooped Kari up and headed for the stairs. He took them two at a time before turning toward the hallway that led to her suite. Then he marched to one of the many doorways she hadn't yet explored.

Brady and Josh trailed right behind them.

At the door, Ford paused long enough for Brady to key in a code. He hesitated on the threshold, staring down at her. "I just want you to know that we've never brought a woman here before. When we designed this place, we knew what we wanted. We just never found it...until you."

Kari's chest nearly exploded with the force of the

emotions swamping her. She was sure now. She was more to them than another temporary lover. No, this was something big. They were investing as much as she was and she refused to reject them again, because if they ever did it to her, it would destroy her. If it was the same for them, she couldn't be responsible for inflicting that kind of pain on people she...loved.

She murmured, "Show me."

Ford kicked the door open and Brady slapped out a hand, so that the heavy paneled wood didn't rebound into them as Ford carried her past it. They kept true to their word, revealing not only the gorgeous space, but the intention behind it. Ford's hold on her knee and shoulder increased despite his trembling fingers.

Could he really be nervous that she wouldn't approve? That their thoughtfulness and long-held intentions wouldn't sway her?

"Each of our rooms connects to this one," Ford told her. "So does your suite. There's a door hidden behind a panel in the bathroom."

"Our idea was that we could have a place to share, and space to ourselves when we need it," Brady filled in for him. "We don't expect you to be with all of us at once all the time. And...well, we sort of each want our own private time, too."

"By that, he means alone time with you. We can still be selfish sometimes, sorry," Ford said with a wink.

What they were suggesting, the kind of life they were proposing, resonated with her. Their vision matched the dreams she'd had for the future. Could it really be like that between them?

God, she hoped so...someday.

For now, there was something else she needed. Something more immediate and primal.

"That's...a lot to think about." She stroked Ford's cheek. Hopefully the gentle touch would communicate how deeply they'd spoken to her. It was exactly what she'd needed to hear.

"Don't worry about all that tonight, okay?" Brady asked as he looked at her over Ford's shoulder. "We can hammer out the details later. We just need you to understand how serious we are."

Kari remembered the night before, when Josh and Ford had tried to say so. She hadn't understood the depths of their desires and that they reached far beyond a few incredible orgasms. Now she did.

She nodded. "The fact that you've put this much thought into it already makes me feel better. I'm sorry I bolted this morning. I should have stayed and listened."

"Should we take a break now? I don't want to make the same mistake again." Josh reached up and squeezed the hand she was using to cling to Ford's shoulder.

"No. I'm ready this time. I know what I'm asking for and...what I'd like to give you." She looked from Josh to Brady and last to Ford. "I want you. All of you. Right now. Together."

Ford's smile was almost predatory. "Then that's what you'll get."

13

Ford tossed Kari onto the biggest bed she'd ever seen, making her laugh as she bounced into the center of it. Sure, he could have treated her like she was fragile or broken. But he didn't. It was an admission that she was strong enough to handle him...no, *them*.

While the guys advanced, she glanced around. The bed was focal point of the room, which was painted a rich gold and furnished lavishly. It was round, and covered with decadent burgundy satin sheets. She felt a little like a sacrifice to some super sex gods.

A very willing sacrifice.

Brady reached her first. He knelt at the edge of the bed then crawled toward her, looking far more like a panther than the gentleman she knew him to be. He was sleek and fierce, his onyx hair tumbling out of place and into his eyes as he approached. She shivered and instinctively spread her legs, wanting to feel him between them.

With a crooked smile, he obliged, though not as directly as she might have wished. He started by kissing the inside of one of her ankles, then slowly traveling upward.

That gave Josh time to join them.

His tactic was less suave and more eager. He leapt onto the bed and skidded across the smooth sheets until he wound up kneeling near her right shoulder. He grinned as he descended, covering her lips with his.

Kari moaned and her spine arched, presenting herself for whatever they wished to indulge in. It said everything about how much faith she had in them, down deep, because earlier that day she would have sworn she'd never have the courage to expose herself again.

And this was a whole new level of intimacy.

Ford surprised her. He took a moment to stand back and watch his friends devouring her. His hand cupped the bulge in his pants, squeezing and rubbing it while his eyelids drooped. There was no doubt he wanted her. Craved this. But he was taking his time as if he knew once he entered the fray, there would be no turning back.

"Let me see you," Kari demanded between Josh's kisses.

Ford reached behind himself and grabbed a fistful of his shirt. He pulled it over his head and threw it aside in one swift movement that made her toes curl even before she admired his lightly haired chest and rock-solid abs. That might also have been in part due to Brady, who had worked his way up to her inner thigh, biting her lightly around the same time.

A hiss escaped Kari. She held her left hand out toward Ford, needing him to complete their group.

He still didn't hurry. This time he unbuttoned his pants, then slid the zipper down carefully to avoid his raging erection. Next he tucked his fingers in the waistband and stepped out of his slacks before folding them and placing them neatly on a chair nearby.

Anticipation was killing her.

The sight of Ford standing there in his boxer briefs, his erection stretching nearly to one hip, had her drooling.

"You want him to take those off?" Josh asked her.

She nodded vigorously.

"Maybe you should tell him what you'll do if he does," Josh prodded her, making her aware of how much he got off on her interactions with his best friends.

"I would suck his cock. I want it filling my mouth, fucking it, so I can taste him." She gasped when Brady rewarded her candor with a kiss on her mound. He nuzzled her there, blowing warm air across her skin before licking a line from her clit to her opening. "Oh, damn. Yes."

Kari shifted, spreading her legs so Brady's broad shoulders could wedge between them. She looked back to Ford then, who was gloriously naked, and curled her fingers toward her palm. "Come here. Please."

Josh lay down next to her and pressed himself to her side. He held her steady, reminding her of all the reasons why this was okay. No, so much more than just okay.

He put his hand over her chest, measuring the pounding of her heart with his fingertips before cupping one of her breasts. "You're so soft and yet so strong. I love that about you, Kari."

He kissed her shoulder and neck, distracting her as Ford came closer.

She tried not to shiver when he said the L-word with that much passion and devotion. Someday she hoped he could fall in love with all of her, instead of admiring certain pieces and parts.

When Ford's knees bumped her left arm, she looked up at him towering over her. If she'd been on her own, she might have gotten scared. But Josh squeezed her to him, wrapping himself around her and stroking her exposed skin from her belly to her ribs and up to her neck, where his fingers rested lightly before returning to her chest. "I've got you, Kari. You're going to love this, okay?"

She nodded, her left hand lifting toward Ford's thick cock, which dangled above her.

"Go ahead," he coached. "Touch me however you like."

Her fingers wrapped around his shaft then weighed his heavy balls in her hand, rolling them around her palm. She sighed as she thought of how he would stretch her open in the not so distant future. But first, she wanted to make him feel as good as he had done for her time and time again.

Kari put her hand around him and tugged until he came closer. She led him by the dick straight to her mouth. Then she painted it with his precome, rubbing the fat head of his cock over her slightly parted lips. Her tongue flicked out to steal a taste of him, lapping at the very tip.

"Fuck, yes," he groaned. "Quit playing and suck me, Kari."

She loved that she could do this to him. To them. Josh stared as Kari opened her mouth, and Ford widened it even further as he slid inside. She sucked around him, drawing him deeper, loving the raw grunts he made as she welcomed him with swirls of her tongue and the barest scrape of her teeth.

Brady must have been impressed. He buried his face between her legs, licking at her folds before using his talented tongue to tease her clit. She shivered, grateful for Josh's tightening hold. He kept her grounded while she lost herself to the dual pleasures of Brady's mouth on her and hers on Ford.

When Brady began to suck lightly on her clit, she redoubled her efforts on Ford, mimicking the motions. "Damn, baby."

His fingers speared into her hair, pulling her tighter to his abdomen. The zing that ran through her scalp made her shudder. Her pussy pulsed. Brady seemed to understand what she needed without being told. The tip of his finger nudged her opening. He pressed against her clenched muscles, boring in until he penetrated the tight ring.

Kari cried out around Ford's dick. She sucked harder, trying to encourage Brady.

"Yes, she loves that. Give her more," Ford rasped to his partner.

Meanwhile, Josh kept murmuring to her, telling her how hot she looked and how he'd never get tired of seeing her unravel. He cooed to her, rubbing his erection against her thigh so she knew every dirty word he whispered was true.

When he dipped his head and took her nipple into his mouth, she quaked in his hold. Having any one of them had surpassed all of her prior sexual experiences. When she'd lost herself between two of them, she had forgotten how to think and surrendered to the overwhelming passion they infused her with. All three...

She didn't stand a chance at holding back. They brought down every wall she'd ever constructed and flooded her with passion and pleasure.

Overwhelmed with emotions and sensation, she

wasn't sure how she could do anything other than bask in it.

Kari opened her eyes and looked up at Ford. He was staring down at her, his hand still cradling her head, keeping her in place as he fed her his thick cock.

"Fuck yes." His hips twitched, making his erection nudge her soft palate. "Watching you loving every moment of this makes me so damn hard."

That was no lie. She moaned around his shaft.

"It's too good. Everything we've ever desired. It's enough that I could lose it right now. Fill your mouth..." He grunted.

Josh lifted his head, letting her nipple slide from his mouth as he stared in shock. "There's no way you're going to come that fast. That never happens."

Even Brady hesitated, which made Kari squirm and chase his fingers with her pelvis. He blinked then sank them back inside her as deeply as he could.

"Today isn't like every other day," Ford grated, his voice husky.

The reassurance that what they had was extraordinary did funny things to Kari. A spasm wracked her. Her pussy hugged Brady deep within her and she thrust her chest up at Josh, who redoubled his attention on her breasts. He pinched the tip of one in time to the gentle nips he placed on the other.

Ford tightened his grip, drawing her attention back to him. "Would you come with me? I'm not alone in this, am I?"

The flash of uncertainty from him—of all people—did her in. It made her feel things for him that she'd never experienced before. Kari relaxed and he slid deep into her throat. Surrounded by heat and so much attention focused on bringing her ecstasy, she was right there with Ford.

She tried to warn him. Though her cry was unintelligible, he got her message even before Brady stopped sucking her clit long enough to tell his best friends that she was clamping down on him.

Kari bucked. The moment Brady's mouth reconnected with her clit, she shattered.

She might have rocketed into space if they hadn't been there to hold her. The spurt of Ford's come in her mouth gave her something to concentrate on. She drained him dry, sucking and swallowing each drop that proved he was in every bit as deep as her in this thing.

Suckling him as he softened gave her comfort and time to return to her senses.

When she did, she realized Brady and Josh had ditched their clothing.

Ford withdrew and collapsed onto a pile of pillows before drawing her into his arms, her back to his chest. He crushed her in a hug that said more than words ever could.

"Will you let me in?" Brady asked, capturing her attention. "Or is it too much…"

"Never." She opened her arms and welcomed him against her. Sandwiched between Ford and Brady, she only experienced longing. Not even a glimmer of panic raced through her when he began to glide his cock up and down the valley at her core. He rubbed himself against her, letting her get used to the feeling for a while before he put his hand between them and angled the tip of his cock so that it began to penetrate.

Kari gasped.

Josh, who was observing from beside them, got to his

knees. His fist pumped his cock as he watched Brady work his way inside her patiently, calmly, and steadily.

She missed the weight and heat Ford had given her and couldn't stand for Josh to feel left out. So she hooked her hand around the back of his thigh and pulled him to her. It was different when he slid between her lips. Less forceful and possessive than Ford had been.

Josh gave her the chance to explore, to play and test the waters. He stayed still while she devoured him, discovering all the things he enjoyed best.

Meanwhile, Brady began to sink into her with the slowest, steadiest strokes she could imagine. He was like a fuck machine, set to make her crazy with a gradual climb toward rapture that could last for hours if she wanted it to.

Damn. Kari shivered in Ford's grasp.

He smiled down at her. "Do you like it like this? So slow and steady?"

Kari figured her eyes rolling back in her head was answer enough. She moaned and clenched around Brady.

Ford groaned. "I could never fuck you like that. I'm not patient enough, and when I get inside you... No. There's no fucking way."

"Don't have to." She pumped Josh's cock as she gave her mouth a rest and tried to make Ford understand with what few functioning brain cells she had left. "I like your style. Theirs too. I like it all. Need different things."

Instead of answering her, Ford leaned in and crushed his mouth over hers. The combination of his rough touch, Brady's consistent, thorough lovemaking, and Josh playing with her breast, encouraging her to let go, made sure she did just that.

Kari erupted around Brady, drawing him into a deep, drawn-out climax along with her. His come felt like magma inside her, a slow, hot flow of thick liquid that seared every place it touched. He flooded her with his release, calling her name while never halting his even, unrelenting thrusts.

Ford cradled her against his solid chest. Her head rested on his shoulder. He hugged her tight from behind. His feet were planted on the bed, spread wide. Her legs draped over them, her thighs being pressed apart by his as Brady withdrew, leaving a pearly line of fluid to decorate her entrance. She knew he did it on purpose, putting her on display for Josh, who stared at her with hungry eyes.

"See how bad he wants your pussy?" Ford asked in her ear. "Do you think you're up for him, too?"

"If he doesn't fuck me right now, I'll never forgive him." Kari reached for Josh and yanked him close. He wasn't graceful like Brady, or aggressive like Ford. He laughed as he tumbled into place between her legs.

Brady wilted, lying beside her and Ford as he caught his breath. Kari couldn't say why she did it, but her hand cupped his softening cock as if to say thank-you for giving her so damn much pleasure. He didn't object, so she gave in to instinct, toying with him while Josh began his turn.

He cursed under his breath when he slipped inside her more easily than his friends had, probably because of the lubrication Brady had left behind.

If that bothered him, he gave no hint of it. Opposite, really—he seemed to firm up within her.

Kari wrapped her legs around his hips, forcing him to ride her with fast, short jabs that ensured his turn would take a lot less time than Brady's had. Despite having come twice already, it seemed they had triggered something within her. Something that turned her ravenous.

She wanted exactly what he was giving.

Kari let her head drop onto Ford's shoulder. He took the opportunity to kiss the shit out of her. Brady hummed beside her and she realized his cock was filling more of her hold.

She must have jerked, her hips rocking against Josh. He slipped from her and groaned when he nudged something that was definitely not her pussy.

"Is that your cock?" Josh asked Ford.

"Sorry, yeah." He dropped one hand, worming it between their bodies to adjust his shaft so that it laid flat against his abs instead of bobbing against Kari's ass and Josh's balls.

Kari groaned, missing the contact and, even more so, the connection between all three of them.

"You're hard again?" Josh asked, seeming unconcerned that Ford had been touching him so intimately.

"Yeah," Ford practically panted. Kari could clearly see the veins near his temple standing out. He wanted her again. Badly. "Of course I am. This is the hottest thing I've ever done in my life. Fuck, even Brady is ready to go again. If we keep going like this, we'll be fucking Kari all night."

While that sounded incredible, she had an even better idea. "I'd rather have you at the same time."

Josh and Brady looked to Ford. His smile was tight. "Are you sure? That's...a lot. Maybe we should work up to that."

"No." Kari rocked her head against him. "Do it. I need it."

He studied her eyes for a few seconds more before nodding.

Then he flipped her as if she weighed nothing, splaying her over Brady's chest.

"Ride him." Ford demanded as he lunged for the edge

of the bed and a chest that sat nearby. From one of the drawers, he withdrew something. Kari couldn't see exactly what since she was settling on her knees over Brady, shaking her hair out of her face as he sank inside her bit by bit.

On his way back, Ford pointed to Josh. "Suck him. He's obsessed with your mouth, you know that, right?"

She hadn't, but the way Josh was tugging on himself as he stared at her lips proved Ford was right as usual.

Kari parted her lips and let Josh inside. She made love to his cock as she glided her pussy along Brady's shaft, guided in gentle arcs by the unwavering grip of his hands on her hips.

"And me..." Ford murmured from behind her now. He pressed one slick, cool finger to her asshole, then began to massage lube into the forbidden flesh. "I've always been an ass man. Have you ever let someone fuck you here?"

She shook her head, thrilling Josh while admitting her innocence.

Ford pressed between her shoulders, leaning her forward. Josh adjusted so his cock never once slipped from between her lips. Ford growled, then smacked her ass, the sound ringing throughout the room even as the tingles of sensation resonated in every bone of her body.

There were a lot of things she experienced first with them. All-consuming lust, wild freedom, blossoming confidence, and—fine, she was willing to acknowledge it if only to herself—undying love.

It was all she could think of when Ford rested the fingers of one of his hands around her throat while the other hand guided his cock to her only remaining opening. He possessed her with such skill and finesse that she hardly noticed any discomfort.

How could she when the three of them were so focused on stoking her pleasure?

Before she realized he'd fitted himself to her entirely, he'd begun to move. At first, Brady and Ford fucked her in perfect sync. Then, as they began to pick up speed and intensity, they alternated filling her and retreating so they could do it again.

Kari screamed their names, vibrating Josh's cock with the force of her rapture.

They held on for what seemed like forever, but no one could ride this sort of white-hot lightning bolt of ecstasy for too long.

She opened her eyes, staring into Brady's hazed ones. He nodded, then grunted, "She's on the edge. Let's push her over."

"I'm there," Josh rasped, the tendons in his neck standing out and the ridge of his veins becoming more prominent.

"Me too," Ford said before biting her neck.

That last show of possession and raw emotion did her in.

Kari came so hard she thought she might black out. She wrung Brady and Ford's cock with her body while her tongue lashed Josh. She tasted the salty splash of his release at the same time Brady and Ford began to pump theirs deep inside her.

Pulses of pleasure rang through her, extending their orgasms even as they enhanced her own.

And when the final twinges faded, they melted into a heap on the bed, inseparably entwined. Not only for that night, but forever.

She hoped.

14

Kari almost didn't recognize herself anymore.

She stood naked in front of the full-length mirror in her suite and took in the woman staring back at her. There wasn't a hint of the bruises she'd gotten from the taxi remaining, though the guys had left a few hickeys and love bites on her otherwise pale skin. Thankfully, they were predominantly on parts of her body she only exposed to them.

A week ago, she'd had no idea she could be this person. Confident. Satisfied. Relaxed. Capable of wearing out three incredible men in bed night after night.

Was it wrong that she liked what she saw so much?

Hell no.

Unfortunately, it also wasn't an entirely accurate representation of who she was. Because, while she'd flourished under their attention, they'd been living in a dream world, cut off from reality. Although Marty still hadn't been caught, she couldn't hide up here in their tower forever.

Especially not on a night as important as this.

Ford, Brady, and Josh were being recognized for their philanthropic leadership in the community. They were the guests of honor at the annual fundraising gala for St. Mary's Medical Center. It meant even more since she'd so recently visited the place and benefited, in part, from their generosity. Despite their reservations about her leaving the shelter of their home, she wanted to be the arm candy they deserved. Not so secretly, part of her also demanded that she stake her claim on them publicly.

Besides, things had reached a standstill in the search for Marty. It might be best to lure him into the open with a very public, very controlled appearance. At least, that's what Bronson had recommended. It had taken a few days, several arguments, and some very persuasive make-up sex for her to convince the guys to take his advice. Eventually, they'd agreed.

Hell, once they'd caved, it seemed Ford, Brady, and Josh were more eager than she was to be seen together. To show her off and take their relationship to the next level. Prove to the world that they weren't afraid of judgment, attack, or any other obstacles the future would fling in the path to their happiness.

Which probably had something to do with her newfound, assured poise.

Now she had to make her appearance match how she felt inside.

It was intimidating as fuck meeting the expectations people would have of her men's significant other. Even if she had been dating just one of the city's most eligible bachelors instead of all three.

They made her feel bold enough to try something she would have dismissed out of hand before. Three sexy, intelligent, kind, and wealthy studs drooling over her was definitely good for her self-esteem. She still couldn't quite believe it was true, though each time they got naked together it sank in a bit more.

Even better, she'd seen something more substantial than lust during the time they spent together. In Brady's refined touches, in Ford's fierce possessiveness, and in Josh's sweet words. They cared for her. Not only as a playmate, but also as a life partner. They wanted to bring her into their group, make her a part of everything they shared.

That inspired her to live up to their standards.

Not because they would be critical of her otherwise, but because they deserved the absolute finest things in life. They made her want to be her best self.

Kari ran her finger over the delicate lace of one of the fancy lingerie pieces she'd found in the dresser with the tags still on. They were from the store she'd shopped at with Andi, and she recognized them from the latest season's collection, which had recently been released. The pieces had obviously been chosen with her favorite colors, and the ones most flattering to her features, in mind. These weren't clothes they'd kept for any overnight guests who might happen by. They'd stocked the room for her and her alone.

Their thoughtfulness did funny things to her guts.

She wanted to embrace it. To show her appreciation and treat herself to a glimpse of what her life could be like if this actually became the forever thing it had the potential to be. If she didn't screw something up. If the guys didn't change their minds. And if Marty and other external forces in the universe left them the hell alone.

Tonight, she was going to let all the *what ifs* go—all the worries and the doubts and the walls she'd built to protect herself—and simply enjoy. If only for a couple of hours.

Suddenly, she felt like she was having another Cinderella moment. They did that to her. Brought out her inner princess and let her play at being their queen.

Kari took a few minutes to figure out the straps and cutouts and fasteners on the frilly lilac contraption, then began to suit up like she was donning feminine armor. Tonight, she was going to be untouchable. She prepared herself to absorb the curious stares that would no doubt lance her from the moment she appeared at the event with the three powerful lawyers.

Many of the attendees were also their clients, so she knew quite a few of them. Would they realize she was attending in something other than an official capacity?

If they saw the way the men looked at her now, openly displaying their desire, it would be obvious. Hell, there had always been those who speculated about their close relationship with their executive assistant in the past. This time they would be right. Well, except for the fact that she no longer worked for them.

With a snap, Kari fastened one garter then the other. Let them look. Let them see what her guys did to her, how they elevated her and, hopefully, how she complemented them.

She stood back to admire herself, already liking what this thing did to her curves. It was flattering and surprisingly comfortable as it conformed to her shape and heat.

It didn't surprise her in the least that one of the guys— Brady, if she had to guess—was this in tune with her. He could anticipate what she needed. And he had excellent fashion sense too.

Turning her back to the mirror, she looked over her shoulder at her ass. Not bad, she thought. All those times she'd forced herself to take the stairs to their office on the top floor were paying off right now.

With a grin, Kari strode to the walk-in closet, which was at least half as big as her bedroom in her own normal-sized apartment. It was loaded with a full wardrobe, including a section with enough shimmer, beadwork, and sequins to blind a girl. She headed straight for that rack.

Kari ran her fingers across the fabrics, tears suddenly prickling her eyes. How would she ever go back to being ordinary if things didn't work out?

She shook her head. *Not tonight. We're not doing that tonight, remember?*

She brushed the moisture from her eyes then got serious about making a selection. They were running out of time and she still had to figure out what to do with her hair and makeup. Hopefully something simple and elegant would suffice.

She had narrowed the choice to a top three when a knock came at the door.

Ford called, "Kari?"

"Go away. I'm not ready yet!" She glanced at the clock. About an hour to go before they had to leave. "Not even close!"

A chorus of male chuckles sounded from the hallway. "I'm not rushing you. Brady thought you might like some help, so he arranged for a personal stylist, who is here waiting to work with you if you'd like."

He what? Kari froze. She'd known Brady was responsible for most of these details. He had the eye for it. And he'd gone even further...for her.

A grin broke out across her face and she sprinted toward the sound of their voices, loving the feel of the opulent carpet beneath her bare toes. She opened the door—just the barest crack—and peeked through. "Hi! I'm a hot mess. Can you help me?"

Ford, Josh, and Brady's eyes widened as they caught a glimpse of her fancy underwear, though not enough to give away all her secrets. The stylist, a young man with a whole lot of flair, pushed past her three imposing guys like they were nothing.

Kari loved him on sight.

He spun around, blocking the sliver of her visible in the doorway, then shooed them away. "No peeking. You'll have to wait for the finished product."

Josh groaned. "Brady, why couldn't you have hired someone to be on our side?"

"I'm definitely #TeamPrettyLady, which you will appreciate later. Now get out of here and let me do what you paid me an outrageous amount of money for. I can already tell I have a lot to work with." The man spun back toward her, ignoring the guys' half-hearted protests as he slipped inside, then grinned before shutting the door in their startled faces. He gave her a quick finger wave. "I'm Anthony. Let's do this."

"For the record—" Brady raised his voice so she could hear him clearly from the hallway. "—you're gorgeous as you are."

She couldn't ignore that. Kari reopened the door enough so that he could see her smile, but not her body. As she searched for her voice, to tell him how much sharing this night with them meant to her, the guys kept up their banter.

"Naked, no makeup," Ford grumbled. "That's how I like you best."

Josh nodded. "For once, I agree with him. Maybe we should stay home tonight."

"No!" Kari shouted. She needed to show them that she could play at their level. Okay, so maybe she was hoping to prove that to herself too. "I'm wearing one of those pretty dresses. We're going to drink champagne, laugh in soft light, and dance to slow music. That's final! Now go away!"

Josh whipped his head around at that. "You're going to have a drink?"

She'd abstained, refusing every drop of alcohol she'd been offered since the night Marty had poisoned her. It was about time she showed her men that she planned to move on. With them.

"Yeah," she whispered.

"That's...great," Ford said quietly before angling away as if he might lose control of his emotions otherwise. He cleared his throat when Josh put a hand on his shoulder and squeezed.

"Hey Kari." Brady rescued them all, bringing them back to someplace less sad and more fun. A slow smile spread across his face. "I'm glad you like the clothes."

"Thank you," she said, afraid if she tried for something more complicated, her tears might resurface.

"You're welcome." He turned and strolled away, leaving her in Anthony's hands.

"You're *always* welcome," Josh added, then joined him, after shoving Ford toward their own rooms.

Would they be wearing tuxes next time she saw them? She thought so. God, she loved it when they dressed up like that. Unlike when they'd attended other formal events in the past, tonight she'd have the right to ogle them openly. Before she'd had to settle for stealing forbidden glances.

Once they were out of eyesight, she closed the door and flung herself at her fairy godfather. She hugged him and dragged him toward the closet. "I'm so glad you're here."

"Me too," he said as he raked her from head to toe with an appreciative stare. "This is going to be pure gold for my portfolio. I hope you don't mind starring in my Instagram feed."

"Who, me?" She paused. Was he joking?

He whistled. "Those guys weren't kidding, you know? You could stop right here and make their nights. I'm sure of it, and women aren't really my thing."

Kari blushed. "Thanks. I don't usually..." She waved up and down at herself.

"You should. Hell, if I looked like that I'd wear it for my boyfriend in an instant." Anthony laughed as he took her elbow and guided her toward the three options she'd laid out. "Show me what you're considering."

Kari was glad to have his expert opinion as she put on a mini fashion show. The moment Anthony zipped her into a floor-length champagne beaded gown with a deep V-neck and straps that turned into a swoosh of fabric—which draped just above her ass, leaving most of her back exposed—she knew it was the one.

Anthony's bulging eyes confirmed it. He snapped some pictures, then started overloading her with talk of highlighters, contouring, bronzers, shimmer, shadow colors, and plenty of terms she didn't understand at all. So she let him whisk her to the vanity to get started on her hair and makeup.

By the time he'd finished, her transformation was complete.

She'd become the person she'd always longed to be, but hadn't known how to access. She looked sophisticated, classy yet undeniably sexy, and influential in a way she'd only dreamed of before.

That was even before she slipped her feet into sparkly four-inch designer heels that made her legs look longer and more toned than they were.

"I'm not going to lie...this might be my masterpiece." Anthony posed her in the ornate gilded chair, then on the bed, then against the wall.

Secure and radiant, Kari went along with it. "You're going to send me those pictures, right? So I can text them to the guys when I'm not around?"

"Oh, hell yes." Anthony snorted. "You're going to give them a run for their money. And we both know that's saying something."

"You don't think it's...weird?" She paused, peeking up at him from beneath the lush lashes he'd applied.

"Don't you dare do that." He wagged his finger at her. "Stand tall and remember you're enough for any man or three. If you care for them and they care for you, tell anyone who doesn't like it to fuck off. I know it's not always easy. Shit, my boyfriend's family still acts like I'm his roommate and someday he'll grow out of this stage and find a proper wife to settle down with."

Kari hugged Anthony then. "You're right—fuck them."

He laughed. "You're going to be fine. Keep your head up and make any doubters jealous as hell tonight."

"I'll do my best." She shook her hands, though the motion didn't do much to dissipate her nerves, then said, "Will you tell them I'll be with them shortly?"

Anthony grinned. "Yep. Take a few deep breaths and give me a minute to clear out. I wish I could see their faces when they spot you coming down those stairs. Make sure you touch up your lipstick before you leave. I'm sure they're going to mess you up at least a little."

Kari laughed, thankful he'd given her a tutorial on doing it herself while he'd applied it. "Good plan."

They hugged one last time, exchanged information, and then he was gone. She knew it wouldn't be the last time they saw each other. But would they meet again like this, or as friends in a café somewhere to reminisce about that one fairy tale night...?

15

J osh leaned against the bar in their living room, trying not to stare at the piano and remember what they'd done there a week or so ago. It had been the most intense sexual experience of his life up until that point, and then they'd nearly blown it afterward.

The past several days had exceeded even that high bar when it came to passion. Now they had to prove that it wasn't all they had together. That they could merge their lives outside of the bubble they'd been fucking in.

Tonight had to be different. They had to show Kari they'd been building the foundation for a lasting relationship. This wasn't an experiment or a phase. They wanted something real with her. Something that would endure through all of life's ups and downs.

She was the woman for them. He knew it—and had known it for quite some time now.

But it was critical that *she* knew it too.

From the first glimpse of her bold, glittering stiletto on the top of the stairs, his hope grew. It was a statement that echoed through him loud and clear. This Kari was the one he'd known was lurking inside their sometimes-mousy assistant from the start. Bless Brady and Anthony for helping her bring it to the surface.

Josh whipped his stare to Brady, then to Ford. The recognition in their gazes settled him. They saw Kari too. The real woman, emerging bit by bit as she descended the marble stairs hugged by the glass half-wall railing. Her hand trailed down the glossy surface as she seemed to float toward them, surrounded by the golden glow of the setting sun that speared through the floor-to-ceiling windows behind her.

Even the dazzling glints off the city's bay in the background couldn't compete with her shine or detract from the spectacle she made as she approached.

The gown she wore hugged every curve and dip of her luscious body. Ones he'd gotten to know and adore over the past week.

Josh swallowed hard. The motion didn't clear the lump in his throat. He mentally recorded each step she took as she neared, knowing he'd replay this moment a million times in his mind during the rest of his life.

"You're absolutely gorgeous," Brady said as he full-on gawked.

"Sexy as fuck," Ford agreed in his more direct manner.

Josh couldn't speak. He cleared his throat, then tried again. Nothing would come out.

Kari laughed as she realized he was literally speechless. "Thank you, Josh. You all look pretty hot yourselves."

Ford charged then, despite their agreement to keep their hands—and dicks—to themselves. He didn't do a very good job of showing her how civil they could be when he crushed Kari to him and devoured her mouth. Brady tapped him on the shoulder.

Ford lifted his head, blinking as if in a daze.

"Oh shit. Sorry." He loosened his hold, making Kari sigh with what seemed like regret. "I couldn't help myself. It was only a taste."

"We're going to be late if we do much more of that." Kari glanced at the watch on Ford's wrist. It was the one Brady had given him for his birthday. "Why don't we get in the car first, and then you can entertain yourselves on the way to the banquet?"

"Did you just proposition us for limo sex?" Josh asked, then snorted. "Because for the record, I am totally down for that."

"Let's go." Ford took Kari's hand in his and laced their fingers. He sped toward the elevator and Bronson, who waited out by the curb.

Kari didn't have any trouble keeping his pace. The long strides made her seem even more glamorous in her mile-high heels and sparkly dress.

During the descent in the elevator, Josh had to blink to keep from being blinded by her. Not all of the brilliance came from what she was wearing. He swore she was glowing from the inside out and he would do anything in his power to keep it that way for the entire night.

The three partners formed a triangle around her when they left the building, even for the short crossing to their limo. Bronson was standing guard, looking in every direction, on high alert despite his calm façade. It wouldn't do anyone any good to forget that despite the epic distraction Kari made, they needed to stay vigilant. There were still plenty of landmines, including that fuckwad Marty, they could stomp on by accident.

Brady held the door for Kari as Ford climbed in first and held his hand out to her. Josh put his palm low on her back as he ushered her inside. Before Kari's ass had even hit the seat, Ford was rolling up the tinted partition between them and Bronson. The guy was more like family than an employee and they rarely used that feature of the car.

That had to be a dead giveaway of what was about to happen. When only a sliver of space remained between it and the roof of the car, Ford instructed, "Drive slowly."

"Yes, sir," the man said with a grin Kari wouldn't be able to miss in the rearview mirror.

What would she think of that?

Josh froze, afraid she would be spooked when she realized that Bronson, and everyone else that saw them tonight, would know exactly what the score was between them. There was no hiding the way he—or the other guys —looked at her. How they touched her, and were about to touch her a whole lot more right then...if she'd let them.

16

Kari laughed when she saw Bronson's smile. She flashed him a thumbs-up right before the dark glass slid into place, granting her and her guys ultimate privacy for the time it took to reach their destination.

Brady shut the door behind him as he perched beside her, with Josh and Ford across from them. The three men were sitting stark still, riveted to her expression, as if she'd just shocked the hell out of them.

"What?" she asked them with a smug smile. "Did you think I'd be embarrassed?"

Josh shrugged one shoulder, as if that was exactly what he'd thought, even if he didn't want to admit it.

"Sorry to disappoint you, but I'm not." Kari licked her lips as she scanned over the three of them. "I'm proud."

Honored that she could be what these three virile, very eligible bachelors wanted...and even seemed to need. So she didn't waste a single second in proving it to them.

Kari slid to the floor of the car. Plush carpeting padded

her knees as she reached a hand out to Ford on her right and Josh on her left.

"Brady, I want you to sit between them." She glanced over her shoulder to make sure he was doing as commanded. When he approached, they played automobile Twister until she had each of them where she preferred them.

"This wasn't exactly what I had in mind..." Ford narrowed his eyes at her.

"Too bad." She sliced her hand through the air. "Shut up, and show me your cock."

Ford growled, then practically ripped his pants open.

"How can you look so sweet yet talk so dirty?" Brady asked appreciatively.

"It's all an illusion." Kari smiled a little sadly. Was she just playing dress-up tonight? Or pretending she knew what to do with these three guys?

Josh laughed. "Nah. I believe the old Kari, the one with her hair in a bun and those ugly suits, was the imposter. You were hiding in there all along."

"Except we see you," Ford told her as he held out his hand to her. "We always have."

She squeezed his fingers. He used their connection to yank her hand to his hard-on. He wrapped her fist around his shaft and threw his head back. "Do whatever you want with me. With us. Later it'll be our turn."

Power flooded her veins. Sure, she might have been the one kneeling before them, but she had absolute authority. She planned to make certain they were every bit as amped up as she was. And she didn't have any intention of relieving the pressure before they returned home that night.

It seemed only fair considering how often she'd

drooled over them during meetings at the office. Besides, the function wasn't that far from their building, in one of the most posh neighborhood of the city. She didn't have enough time to see to each of them properly.

Kari looked at Josh and then at Brady, who were observing her pumping Ford's cock. She lifted one perfectly arched brow at them, then asked, "Why aren't you two being as good as Ford?"

"Oh. Right." Josh swallowed hard as he undid his pants, but he never took his eyes off the spot where her flesh met Ford's. "He always was the smart one."

Brady hummed. "I like this side of you."

"Good, then show me how much. Do as I say." Kari gestured with her chin to the front of his bulging pants. It turned her on to see their formalwear in perfect order from the waist up and their stiffening cocks jutting from beneath crisp white shirts.

She couldn't help but pause for Josh and Brady to finish situating themselves. So she used her free hand to sneak beneath the thigh-high slit in her dress and rub her pussy through the delicate lace of her underwear. Of course, that didn't help alleviate the ache there in the least.

"I can have Bronson take a detour," Ford told her.

"No." She shook her head. "It'll be better if we wait until we're home again."

"Can I object?" Josh groaned and banged his head on the window hard enough that she winced. "On the grounds that I might die before then."

"Being horny won't kill you." Brady laughed at his friend's antics. "It will be fun to see you squirming beneath the dinner table, though. If I have to suffer, so should you."

Kari shut them all up when she retracted her hand from under her dress. She held her fingers up to Josh, who didn't hesitate. First he smelled them, inhaling the blended scent of her arousal and the fancy perfume they'd placed in her room. It was intoxicating, even to her.

Then he leaned forward and took the digits into his mouth. He sucked on them. The resulting zing of sensation reminded her of what she had in store for them. If she didn't hurry, she'd miss her chance to play the seductress for once.

While Josh swirled his tongue around her fingers, she leaned forward and nuzzled Brady's shaft and balls. Her other hand tightened on Ford, using the pad of her thumb to stroke the underside of his cock. She withdrew her wet fingers from Josh's mouth and treated his cock to a simultaneous massage.

"Son of a bitch!" he growled at the ceiling of the limo.

Ford, however, was watching her. He hardly blinked, preferring instead to study her as she manipulated all three of them at once. Admiration shone from his gaze, and his cock hardened fully in her grasp. He was turned on by her assertiveness, appreciative of her taking initiative.

She angled her face so she could lip Brady's balls before kissing her way from the base of his shaft up to the tip. When her mouth settled over his cockhead and she began to suck, Brady moaned. His hands flew to his seatbelt as if he was afraid he might launch out the moon-roof of the limo.

"That feels incredible," he rasped.

"I know. She sucked the hell out of me on the piano the other night." Ford's bragging did something to her. It stoked the fire burning within her and encouraged her to be even more forward, even more brave.

Josh grunted. "I remember. That was...amazing. So is this. More, Kari."

She obliged him, speeding up the glide of her fist over his length. The upward thrust of his hips knocked into the side of her hand as he pushed through the ring of her fingers, enhancing her motions. "Sit still, Josh. Take what I give you. Don't be greedy."

Ford laughed. "You're a little *too* good at this, I think."

"You don't like what I'm doing?" She added a twist of her wrist at the top of her strokes so that her palm brushed the sensitive ridge of his corona.

"I definitely did not say that." He stared directly into her eyes when he admitted, "I could come already."

"Don't you dare." She shocked even herself when she instinctively removed her hand and slapped his cock, just enough to get his attention.

Except it only seemed to make him harder. A bead of precome emerged from the tip of his dick and rolled downward. She hummed as she descended on Brady again.

It was the next best thing to tasting Ford.

Brady groaned. "If you think *he's* about to shoot..."

Kari stole his ability to speak when she relaxed her throat, dropped her jaw, then let him deep inside. She swallowed around him while her hands mimicked the treatment as best they could on Josh and Ford.

All three guys went silent.

It was kind of a miracle, really.

Kari smiled around Brady's cock as she spent the next several minutes trying to give them even a fraction of the pleasure they'd bestowed on her the past week, each night they'd spent together in their shared room. It still seemed like a dream. An indulgent, naughty, wicked dream.

The slight soreness in her thighs and the ache in her pussy told her it had been very real.

She couldn't wait to do it again.

Just the thought of them taking turns filling her, fucking into her from over, under, and behind made her wanton. She sucked harder while her hands flew over Josh and Ford's shafts.

A bead of sweat trickled down Brady's forehead. His feet drummed on the floor.

A few more seconds...

"Kari, stop," Ford grumbled, nudging her shoulder until Brady's cock slipped from her mouth with a moist pop.

"Why? Are you going to come?" She smiled then, hoping she could push him right up to the edge again.

"I could, but you don't want me to, so I'm holding out." Ford tucked himself back into his pants, then leveled a stare at the other guys. "We're here. You'd better put those away unless you want to make the front page of every tabloid in a *true* story, for once."

As they rolled to a stop, Josh and Brady scrambled to tame their dicks enough to get their tuxes to fit. Kari reluctantly released them, then slid onto the seat behind her, trying to catch her breath for a moment before facing the crowd.

The fact that Bronson didn't immediately come open the door made Kari love him even more than she already had.

"Did you enjoy yourself, baby?" Ford asked as she reapplied her lipstick then gave her face one last check in her compact mirror before tucking it back into her purse.

She nodded, a grin curling one side of her mouth. "Of course. I think I screwed myself over too, though. I'm so wet. And turned on…"

"We still have five minutes before we're officially late," Brady said somewhat innocently, although his implication was anything but.

"There's no reason we should all suffer," Josh added.

"Lift your dress up. Let us see how much you liked touching us. Tasting us. Teasing us…" Ford commanded. Suddenly, he had resumed control, and she didn't want to deny him.

So she did as he said. She walked the luxurious fabric upward until it bunched around her waist. Then she spread her legs, showing them exactly what she had on underneath.

"You look incredible wrapped in lace," Brady sighed.

"This is not helping my cock go down any." Josh stared as she ran her fingers beneath the edge of her panties and over her mound, letting them come to rest over her clit.

"Go ahead," Ford told her. "Make yourself come."

When Kari pressed her swollen bud, she knew it wasn't going to take very much effort. She admitted, "I'm already close."

"Really?" Josh wondered. "You liked touching us that much?"

How could he doubt it? Any lingering speck of awkwardness evaporated. She scooted down in the seat, planted one of her fancy shoes on Josh's knee and the other on Ford's, pushed aside the crotch of her panties, and slid two fingers inside herself.

The other hand began to rub circles around her clit. She closed her eyes and bit her lip to keep from screaming their names. When Ford's hand wrapped around her ankle like a living manacle and squeezed, she unraveled.

Kari came while they watched, her body undulating as it usually did while they were inside her.

"Yes, that's right," Ford murmured.

Brady sighed, "Fuck, you're gorgeous."

And Josh... Well, he jerked in his seat, grunting several times in close succession.

"Dude, did you just—?" Brady whipped his stare to Josh.

"Anyone have a handkerchief?" he asked with a grin, after a few moments of harsh breathing. His face seemed as flushed as hers felt.

"I wanted you hard and horny," Kari said, pouting despite the fact that she was floating on her own euphoric cloud.

"Don't worry, I will be." He grimaced. "I haven't come in my pants since I was a teenager. That's not going to be enough to flush this out of my system."

They took another minute or two to get their shit together and make themselves appear respectable. Then Ford let Bronson know they were ready to go. He came around and opened the door, letting Josh out first, then Brady. Ford gestured for her to go next, with him bringing up the rear.

Though they'd had a hell of a time, they hadn't forgotten the dangers tonight held as well as the pleasures. They were vigilant, despite her earlier diversions.

Kari took Bronson's hand, grateful that he held her steady as she emerged from another fantasy. While she might have been shy in the past, she could only beam when he handed her from the vehicle and said, "Have fun tonight, Ms. Hill."

"I'm sure we will. Thank you."

"Bronson, stay close in case we decide to leave early tonight. I have a feeling we're not going to make it very late into the evening before home sounds too good to resist." Ford shook the man's hand before taking hold of Kari's elbow. He guided her toward the red carpet and the slew of photographers awaiting them.

17

A divine dinner topped off by decadent chocolate raspberry cake satisfied Kari's stomach. Touching speeches by decent people who cared about leaving the world a better place than they'd found it warmed her heart and restored some of her faith in humanity. But her absolute favorite part of the gala was the dancing.

Being whirled around the parquet wood floor by Brady in a decent imitation of a ballroom hold or shaking it between Ford and Josh—either was fine with her. They'd taken plenty of turns, making a spectacle of themselves until her hair had begun to slip from its pins and tendrils had curled along her shoulders.

She paused for a breather next to a piano that didn't look nearly as grand as the one in their living room. The guys' living room, she mentally corrected herself.

"I heard you were good on the piano." Josh winked. "Maybe you should give all those people staring at you a show."

Kari blushed and somewhat discreetly scratched her eyebrow with her middle finger.

The pure sound of his laughter echoed through the room, drawing more than a few glances. Some were curious, some less than kind. Most, Kari noticed in her sweep of the guests around them, seemed to be shooting her envious looks. As they should be. She would have no problem telling any of the women drooling over her guys precisely how incredible they were in bed, and out of it too.

After her long hiatus from drinking, Kari knew she'd had too much expensive champagne. Not because the world had spun a bit when Brady twirled her around the dance floor a few dances ago, but because she had to pee. Bad.

It meant something to her that she'd indulged, even if the guys couldn't totally comprehend what a monumental step it was for her to trust anyone—*them*—so much again. No matter what, they would take care of her. She didn't have a single shred of doubt about that.

"Would you excuse me for a second? I need to use the ladies' room," she whispered in Josh's ear before stepping away from his chest.

"Want me to walk you there?" he asked.

"No thanks. I'm fine." She smiled softly up at him, annoyed that her past was interjecting itself in the evening, trying to tarnish her future. There was no way Marty could get to her here. It was far too public, and the guest list too exclusive for him to sneak past security.

"I'll be back at our table with Ford and Brady," he told her. "I think they'll be handing out awards soon, and then we can go."

Kari nodded, trying to cross her legs subtly. She

probably should have quit a couple flutes ago or maybe a couple of dances ago, but nothing had salved her pride so much as the freedom to indulge in a while. Well, other than sex with Ford, Josh, and Brady, but that was hardly a fair standard for anything else to stack up against. That had been spectacular, but in a whole other way. This was a light, floaty feeling. One she desperately needed after all the heavy shit that had bombarded her life lately.

"Be right back."

"I'll miss you," he said, then kissed her cheek. She wondered how many people noticed. Did they think she was his date? Or did they know—as she'd previously learned from whispers—that the three men liked to share their women?

Would they think the guys had lost their minds choosing her, of all people, to shower with affection and attention?

Kari stood tall as she wound through the crowd. She didn't give a shit. All that mattered was what her boyfriends thought. Was that what they were? Her boyfriends? Lovers?

It didn't seem like a serious enough term for how she felt about them, but she figured it would do for right then.

Kari opened the heavy door to the immaculate bathroom. Each toilet had its own tiny individual room, so she chose one and wrestled her dress out of the way so she could use the facilities. With its gleaming fixtures, rich wood paneling, and actual plush towels instead of the paper sort, the restroom was swanky on a whole other level from what she was used to. It was quiet, not overcrowded like at some benefits she'd attended in the past while representing the firm. This was an exclusive gathering of people who expected and got the best.

So when she set her dress back in place and exited the stall, she was surprised to see another woman lounging on a couch in front of a mirror near the sinks. The woman was applying blood-red lipstick with practiced precision. No mirror needed.

Maybe she could teach Kari some of her lady-skills. She opened her mouth to say something to that effect, friendly and complimentary, when the woman turned and Kari realized it had been an artfully sprung trap.

"So I see you're with Ford, Brady, and Josh."

"I came with them, yes." Kari didn't clarify their relationship. Partly because she still didn't know how they were defining it for themselves.

"It's more than that. Everyone can tell when a woman shares their bed. Just don't get used to it."

"Jealous?" Kari couldn't believe she said that. It had slipped out. But her guys were worth fighting for. Staking a claim on. Even if she didn't truly have the right.

It was then that something caught at Kari's memory. Maybe the hand propped on the woman's bony hip, like she had famously posed on a magazine cover. She knew this bitch. The swimwear model. Of course. "They're done with you, Melody. Time to accept that."

"So they still talk about me?" Melody perked up. If she were a cat, her claws would have extended as she went on the attack.

"Hardly." Kari rolled her eyes. "I...used to work for them when they dated you."

"Oh, sweetie. We didn't date. We fucked. A lot." Melody tapped her gold nails on the counter then. "There's no way you could satisfy them like I did. Weren't you their secretary? How trite."

"I haven't had any complaints so far." Kari shrugged

and turned to go, trying not to let the woman reawaken her own insecurities. Melody was gorgeous, sophisticated, and successful in her own right. She matched them—on the outside, at least.

"Except for that guy on the internet who said you were a limp fish in bed." Melody actually had the gall to laugh. She cackled while part of Kari died inside. What man?

"What the fuck are you talking about?"

Kari's carefully constructed armor clearly had a chink in it. She exposed the hint of her vulnerability and Melody pounced all over it. "The one who fucked you in that alley at the law firm's Christmas party last year. How trashy are you? Sure, Ford, Brady, and Josh want someone exotic and daring. But they don't want trash. Maybe I should text them the link? I'm sure they're not going to be flaunting you once they realize you spread your legs for the entire staff before working your way up to their executive offices."

The woman pulled her phone from her purse. She tapped and swiped with a few surgical motions that made Kari sure she had the video keyed up in advance. At the first bit of audio of Marty cajoling her into the alley with him, Kari lost it.

Her legs gave out and the buzz from her drinks turned into poison in her guts. She grabbed for the counter but missed, then crashed into a pile on the floor.

Every second was torture. She relived the memories she had blanked from her mind. They came rushing back with each horrific moment Melody replayed like it was nothing.

Kari put her hands over her mouth, but they couldn't hold in her screams.

"Shit." Melody rushed over, pale. "Get yourself together. I won't really show them."

More screams. Kari couldn't make it stop. She hadn't been able to make it stop then and the phone just kept playing that atrocious movie, reminding her of everything Marty had taken from her.

Melody reached for Kari, but she crab-walked backward, smacking her head on the sink in the process. An inhuman sound—one of fear and pain—bubbled up from inside her. She couldn't make it stop.

"Oh shit." Melody ran from the restroom, shouting for help.

Kari couldn't say how long she sat there, sobbing and trying not to be sick.

Next thing she knew, Ford plowed through the restroom door, making it smash into the wall in his haste to get to her. He skidded across the floor on his knees and gathered her into his arms. Unlike when Melody had reached for her, his protective hold didn't disturb her in the least.

"Kari! What's wrong?" He rocked her, trying to stifle her cries.

Brady and Josh were only a few steps behind. Melody poked her head inside, then tried to slink away.

"That cunt!" Kari stabbed her finger in Melody's general direction.

"What did you do to her?" Brady demanded as he approached the other woman. Kari had never been afraid of him, not for a single moment, but she would have been if he'd aimed that much anger and revulsion at her.

"I'm sorry. Things got out of hand. I was just..." Melody looked away, obviously rattled by Kari's psychotic reaction.

"Being a petty bitch?" Josh asked. "We've told you—it's over. Don't you dare come near Kari again."

"V-video," Kari choked out as she buried her face in Ford's jacket. Humiliated, shocked, and drowning in agony all over again. She hated that they would see it. But they had to in order to help her. To bring an end to all of this, once and for all.

"What is she talking about?" Ford shouted at Melody.

"Here." Melody held her phone out to the guys. "Here. Take this. I think I misunderstood. I thought it was funny. A publicity stunt, since it was posted on the internet. The guy said he didn't deserve to get fired for it and she was spreading lies about him. But maybe I had this all wrong... I didn't mean to..."

"What the hell is this?" Brady jammed his finger on the screen, causing Marty's voice to cut through again.

Kari wailed and clutched Ford as she heard her own slurred voice. She remembered the bruising impact of his cold, clammy hands on her as he'd pressed her against the building. Bile rose in her throat again.

"Turn that the fuck off!" Ford roared.

"Oh God. No." Josh wilted, sinking to his ass on the floor as though he might join her in her weeping. "How could you?"

"I'm sorry," Melody whispered. "I'm so sorry. I didn't realize. I thought you were drunk and having a good time."

"Get the fuck out of here, and never contact us or her again." Brady ripped the door open and glared until Melody slunk out.

It took more than a half hour before Kari was able to stand up again. After she got to her feet, dusted herself off, and verified her jellied knees would hold, she made sure that she walked from the bathroom on her own two feet.

Yes, Ford held her hand in an iron grip, Brady had his arm curled around her waist, and Josh fended off anyone who might approach, even with the best of intentions, as they made their way to the car.

But she did it with her head held high and dared anyone to think that she couldn't survive.

Marty had hurt her, but he hadn't broken her.

And he wouldn't.

Her terror and tears turned into righteous rage.

They had him by the balls now. If only they could find the fucker.

18

Kari was sandwiched between Brady and Josh, clinging to their hands while Ford walked out in front of them. Despite the fact that Marty himself hadn't made an appearance, Ford's gaze swung from side to side, confirming their path to the waiting limo was clear.

She had long passed the terrified stage and the sick phase of her shock. Now she was plain exhausted. When they piled into the car, Kari melted against Brady. He tucked her close to his side.

"We'll be there in ten minutes or less," Bronson promised, then hustled around to slide behind the wheel.

Kari hated that she felt compelled to ask, but she had to do it. "You're sure you don't mind me crashing a while longer?"

"I was kind of hoping you'd stay forever." Brady put his hand on her knee and squeezed. He might have been teasing. His words still made her insides do funny things.

"We already knew Marty was evil," Ford said, his voice

pure steel. "Nothing that happened tonight changed my mind about that or what I want our future to look like."

"Mine either," Josh added.

Relief overwhelmed Kari then. She wasn't sure if she slept or sat in a daze, content in the safety of their presence, but she figured it was probably the former because she didn't quite realize they were home until Brady scooped her up and handed her out of the car to Ford.

"I can walk," she mumbled, pushing half-heartedly against his chest.

"You could, but you don't have to." He shielded her with his body as he crossed the sidewalk into the front of their building, protecting her even in that brief moment of exposure.

She didn't protest again, burying her face in his neck so she didn't have to see the worried glances of the front desk staff or the total wreck she must look like reflected back at her in the elevator paneling.

Josh and Brady followed somberly, everyone low-key as they made their way upstairs.

When Ford took her to her private suite, she had to choke back another sob. This was absolutely not how she'd envisioned the rest of their evening when they'd first crammed into the limo earlier.

He set her down near the bathroom. Kari hesitated before pointing toward the door into their shared quarters. "Can we sleep in there tonight?"

"Definitely," Ford said as Brady nodded vehemently.

Josh kissed her shoulder. "I wasn't looking forward to being alone tonight either. After everything that happened, I don't want to let you go."

She knew that feeling. So she held out her hand and he took it.

Ford opened the adjoining door. "Do you need anything else from in here first? Pajamas? A shower?"

Kari looked from the guys to the giant soaking tub and back to the guys. While it was a toss-up as to which sounded more rejuvenating right then—their arms wrapped around her or a long, hot bath—she thought just maybe she might be lucky enough to score both.

"I feel kind of...dirty...after everything that happened." She sighed as she scanned down herself and the gorgeous dress that had torn during her fiasco. "Would you mind if I took a bath before bed?"

Brady shook his head. "Of course not. Would you like us to rummage up a late-night snack? Or maybe a glass of wine?"

"That sounds amazing." She got bolder, asking for what she really wanted. "But only if you'll share it with me. In there."

Ford looked at her, then at the bathtub. "I know that thing's a monster, but if that's what you really have in mind, you should try out the Jacuzzi out on the roof terrace with us."

"You have a Jacuzzi and you haven't mentioned it before?" She kicked off her shoes, groaning as her feet flattened out into something approaching a normal shape. "Does it have jets?"

"Of course." Josh grinned. "I've heard they're almost as good as my mouth, too."

She smacked him lightly with the back of her knuckles. "Not for that. I could use a massage."

His smile faltered, something she hated being

responsible for. So she tried to make it up to him. "Unzip me?"

He did, helping her shuck the dress. All three of the guys went quiet then.

"Oh yeah. I wore this..." She waved at her lingerie. "I have bad luck with this stuff. Maybe I should stop trying to impress you guys with it and go commando instead."

"I don't have a problem with that plan." Ford smiled.

Brady cleared his throat. "There a privacy screen around the pool deck. The reason you couldn't see the Jacuzzi is because that area is covered with vines and flowers. It's pretty sweet, actually."

Josh told her, "What he's saying is that no one will be able to see us out there if you decide you'd rather skip the bikini."

"In that case..." Kari unwound the satin and lace from around her body then strode from the bedroom completely naked. It felt right to take back some of the empowerment she'd felt stripped from her while she was forced to relive her abuse at Marty's hands. It was crazy that she hadn't even realized this was what she needed, and still they were giving it to her. "Follow me, gentlemen."

"I'm feeling anything but civil right now," Ford warned her with a growl. "It might be better if I stay put. You've already had a rough night without me pawing at you, especially when I'm on edge."

"You're coming." Kari grabbed his tie and led him from the room.

"That would probably help." He flashed a grin that did everything to restore her confidence and nothing at all to frighten her despite his concerns.

19

An hour earlier, Brady never would have imagined their night could have made this big of a recovery. From soul-crushing betrayal to skinny-dipping under the stars with Kari, an expensive bottle of wine, and his best friends.

Damn, he was glad it had.

Kari's resilience and her survivor spirit impressed him as always. It helped his heart unclench itself after what they'd heard and seen. He stretched out his arms along the edge of the steamy pool, aligning the jets so they massaged his spine and ass.

It had been one hell of a day. They needed to relax and unwind.

He took another branch of grapes off the platter nearby and ate a couple before noticing Kari watching him. "Want some?"

She nodded and opened her mouth.

Damn. That did nothing to calm his half-hard cock.

Brady leaned forward, plucking one from the bunch

before slipping it between her lips. Eyes closed, she savored the sweet taste before humming. "More."

Who was he to deny her request?

Brady fed them to her one at a time until there were none left, then asked, "Cheese?"

She nodded.

Something about serving her was getting to him. She nipped his fingers when she took the fontina from them.

Meanwhile, Josh took her mussed hair down pin by pin, running his fingers through it as he released the soft waves, which flowed out behind her on the bubbling water. She looked like a siren, except Brady knew the only things she would lure him into would be happiness and a bone-deep satisfaction the likes of which he'd never experienced before.

Even when they weren't setting the sheets on fire, being together with these people made him satisfied. She was it. Everything they'd always wanted.

He looked up at Ford and caught his friend smiling softly, probably thinking the exact same thing. For hyper-ambitious men like them, it was a relief.

Josh finished unraveling her hair, then leaned down for a kiss.

"Thank you," she whispered.

Brady knew she was talking about a lot more than grooming. He answered for Josh, who, for once, seemed unable to find a joke to crack. "We haven't done anything yet. I swear, Kari, we're going to make sure Marty goes away. For as long as technically possible. He will not touch you again. We have more than enough to build our case now. As soon as we find him..."

"I know." Her smile was tight, but her statement held conviction. She trusted them and that meant everything to him. In her situation, he wasn't sure he could be as brave as she was.

Ford pulled them from the dark mood. He asked Josh, "Why don't you show her the massage bench?"

"What's that?" she wondered.

She was about to find out. Brady smiled as Josh locked his arms around her and floated her over to a shallow section of the whirlpool. It was a horizontal shelf molded to cradle a person, complete with a built-in foam pillow. It was also chock full of jets that pulsed, swirled, and kneaded muscles into limp noodles. After difficult days in the courtroom, that thing could work wonders on his tension.

Hopefully, it would do the same for her.

The moment she was in position, Ford tapped a button on the control panel.

Kari's eyes widened, then she hummed. "Oh. That's...wonderful."

"I can make it even better," Josh promised. "Here..."

He sat at the bottom of the bench and plunged his hands beneath the surface of the pool. Kari gripped the side of the Jacuzzi with a gasp as Josh began to rub her feet. Ford and Brady moved closer without a word.

Despite the pillow the water sometimes still splashed in his face when he had the jets cranked up like they were now, so Brady took up a spot near Kari's head and elevated it with one hand. He used his other to rub her shoulder and then up her neck. She shivered in his hold.

Ford split the difference, kneeling near her hip. In the moonlight, it was easy to see the lush curves of Kari's body through the very shallow water. Nothing was obscured. Every now and again her breasts would emerge completely from the humid pool.

It would have been impossible not to notice how hard her nipples were.

Because of the contrast between the cool night air and the warm water? Or because her body was reacting to the plethora of sensations bombarding it?

Brady leaned down and brushed his lips over hers. He crooned to her, "Relax, Kari. We've got you."

Her eyes fluttered closed and she went limp, confident that they did. She couldn't have been more perfect.

Ford, Josh, and Brady showed her how much they appreciated her surrender. They lavished attention on every part of her body until her sighs morphed into light moans. It took a long time to get her there, and even longer to help her enjoy it.

But eventually, she grasped Ford's hand and squeezed. "What do you want?" he asked.

"Each of you, inside me. One by one." She bit her lip. "Make it last. As long as you can. Please. I never want this to end."

They put all their experience to work, giving her what she desired most. Hours passed while each of them spent time inside her, rotating when it became too much for them, trying to erase her bad memories and make plenty of sweet, sensual ones to replace them with.

They did their best to heal her through their physical connection.

It was literally their pleasure to do so.

By the time Kari slipped into a long, languid orgasm that seemed to echo through her body forever, Brady was spent and so were his partners.

They lifted Kari from the whirlpool, toweled her dry, then took her upstairs to their shared suite where they snuggled together and exchanged long, sweet kisses, the rest of the world forgotten entirely.

He wasn't sure who said it first, but when he heard one of his friends murmur, "I love you," into the darkness, he immediately admitted the same truth, then held his breath.

Unfortunately, the only response from Kari was a soft, adorable snore.

20

——————

Marty couldn't believe it. He'd nearly given up. Listened to his family, who were *concerned* about him—as if they'd ever cared before— and the shrink they'd hired to attend the "intervention" they'd staged.

More like an ambush.

Sure, he'd gone overboard with the pills and his drinking. Who could blame him after losing so damn much? His career, his cash, and a woman he'd tried over and over to woo—all of it was gone.

He'd almost agreed it was time to start over and try to do better.

After coming back home and realizing his old firm had sent a take-down request to have his video stripped from the internet, he'd thought it was a sign that his family was right. Kari had gone home with his ex-bosses. They'd retreated into their impenetrable tower, where he couldn't reach them, seemingly unfazed by what he'd tried to show them and the rest of the world about how

Kari had belonged to him first. Before they'd stolen her away.

Game over.

Then, as he'd been about to pack up his surveillance equipment, which allowed him to spy on them from this secret second apartment he could no longer afford, movement had fluttered on the screen that had been empty for days.

It had cost Marty the last of his savings to bribe a maintenance worker into "accidentally" knocking a panel out of the damn privacy screen surrounding the terrace, but it was about to pay off.

Those bastards were getting it on in their hot tub like the freaks they were. They tried to make *him* out to be the bad guy, the pervert, when *they* were obviously getting off on what he'd shown them about Kari.

It was one thing to know they'd had her. To see it…

They'd ruined her. They'd ruined everything.

So he gathered the evidence he needed to make the foursome suffer like he had. He would mutilate their reputations too. Ford, Brady, and Josh were too proud to let a woman destroy the empire they'd built. They'd ditch her as fast as all the other women they'd burned through since he'd known them.

When they cast out Kari, she would come crawling back to him.

Even better, maybe they could convince the lawyers to buy up all the rest of the footage he had to keep from making things worse. Then all his problems would be solved.

With a huge grin, Marty shook the last of his pills into his hand, washed them down with the shitty gin he'd scrounged from the back of his cabinet and shoved his pants down to enjoy the show properly.

21

The next morning, Josh stormed into the penthouse, his fists shaking. In one, he clutched the forgotten bag of food that had been intended to stave off the ravenous hunger brought on by the previous night's sex marathon. In the other...

It was the thing that could bring them crashing down from the pinnacle they'd reached together only hours before. This one piece of crumpled paper had the power to ruin everything. Probably already had. They just hadn't known it yet.

He thought he might puke. The smell of the eggs in the takeout containers revolted him now.

Dashing into the kitchen, he hurled the bag onto the counter, sending hash browns flying.

"Hey, careful with my breakfast," Brady teased. "After last night, I need all the calories I can get."

On the other hand, Kari went on instant alert. She knew him well enough that she could tell something was seriously fucked. "What's wrong?"

She rose from where she was sandwiched between Josh and Ford on the couch and jogged over to him. It said a lot that he hardly noticed the way her breasts bounced in the skimpy satin nightgown she'd put on.

Ford wasn't far behind her. He glanced down at the glossy tabloid Josh's hand was clamped around and cursed. "What's in there?"

Josh winced. This was going to hurt Kari. There was no way around it either. She was going to find out. From him, right now, or from a stranger if he didn't man up and show her.

So he broke the news as gently as he could. "Someone saw us. Together. And they..."

Shit, he couldn't say it when her eyes were so big and wide and innocent on his.

Ford snatched the magazine out of his hand and looked at it for himself. "Motherfucker! They took pictures of us fucking and sold them to this piece-of-shit gossip rag."

Josh nodded. "It gets worse."

"How the hell could it get worse?" Brady roared as he took in the grainy images of the four of them in the hot tub. The juiciest bits were hazy but what was happening was clear as day. Right on the cusp of what the magazine could get away with on the newsstand.

"There's another video online with the promise of more to come. All the major celebrity gossip sites blogged about the scandal and people are out there hunting the links down so hard several of the sites hosting it crashed from the traffic. It's fuzzy but it's obviously us. In the Jacuzzi." He hung his head. "I'm so sorry, Kari. We can go after them, sue them, but that won't take it back. It's out there now. I never thought..."

"How is that even possible?" Ford shouted, then sprinted outside. He cursed loud enough for them to hear even through the sound-deadening glass when he noticed a hole in their privacy screen. It hadn't been visible in the dark the night before.

Only one person could be behind this. The question was, had Marty taken advantage of a pre-existing flaw, or had he created it himself?

Josh's skin crawled. Kari wasn't protected here, with them, despite how many times they'd promised her she would be.

When Ford stormed back inside, Kari flew to him and crushed him in a hug. "Calm down. It's not your fault."

She was consoling them? Josh shook his head, feeling like their whole world had been flipped upside down. Maybe it was because she wasn't a lawyer and she hadn't considered the repercussions.

Ford exchanged a glance with Josh and Brady. All three of them were grim as fuck because they knew exactly how their opposition would use this information. Those bastards would twist this to their advantage. They'd smear Kari and paint her as an immoral woman who'd sleep with anyone, especially multiple people at a time.

While that had absolutely no bearing on whether or not she'd given Marty her consent that night in the alley —and she had certainly never encouraged him to enter her apartment—not everyone would see it that way.

They'd cracked the door for Marty to weasel his way free of the cage they'd been about to nail him into. The man had been one hell of a lawyer, otherwise they never would have hired him in the first place. Because of them,

Kari was going to lose her case. And then she'd never truly be safe.

Josh went cold all over.

Ford's hands fell away from Kari. She blinked up at him, tipping her head to the side as she read his expression. "Oh no. You're not going to let this come between us."

He stepped away from her. So did Brady. And Josh. It was the hardest thing he'd done in his life, making that foot move and then the other until he'd put some distance between them. But it had to be done.

Kari whipped her stare from him to Ford and then to Brady, watching each of them retreat simultaneously.

Josh swore he saw her heart shatter in her chest. Her face warped into a mask of horror and outrage. It felt like the worst sort of infidelity to rescind every promise he'd made to her and leave her out there alone, hurting and afraid.

"Guys?" She put her hand out. None of them took it.

Ford took a deep, shaky breath, then said, "As your lawyer, I'm advising you that it would be best to end this relationship and stay far, far away from here. From us. At least until Marty is caught and his trial is over...and probably forever."

Brady hunched over as if Ford had driven a stake into his heart. Still, he didn't argue. Instead, he nodded. "He's right. In fact, we should resign as your council also. We'll find another qualified firm to represent you."

Josh agreed with his partners. "Kari, you should go."

He couldn't even offer to call Andi or Cooper to come get her, because they were involved in this whole mess too.

Ford said, "Tell Bronson to take you to a secure location. Somewhere we don't know about."

She would be alone, but protected from the collateral damage that came along with being too close to them.

It was for the best.

22

Kari reeled, her heart stomped into mush. She staggered toward the door, clutching her chest. She was less afraid that Marty could be lurking out in the shadows somewhere than she was of the nightmare that had just unfolded inside the lost sanctuary of Ford, Josh, and Brady's penthouse.

Despite the shit show, the guys would certainly have Bronson meet her in the lobby and escort her somewhere she could hunker down until this was finally resolved. Were they right, though? Would this incident never be entirely behind her?

What if Marty got off the hook—despite all the things he'd done to her—because of what others thought of the non-traditional relationship she'd flaunted between her, Ford, Brady, and Josh?

She knew there were plenty of people who wouldn't understand. They would make assumptions about how she viewed intimacy and assume she was willing to go crazy with anyone. What was a little sex up against an alley wall at a Christmas party when you were happy to fuck all three of your bosses too?

Kari's finger trembled as she pressed the elevator button. Going down had never seemed so literal in all her life. Every floor that passed sank her deeper into a pit of despair.

When the doors opened and she practically tumbled out into the lobby, she was both glad and appalled to see Bronson waiting for her. Instead of hauling her by the wrist and rushing her out to the waiting limo, he approached carefully, as if she was a wounded animal. "Kari..."

She couldn't say what made her do it, but she flew at him then, clinging to the poor guy as she began to wail. He hugged her gently and patted her back. "Everything's going to be all right."

"How?" she sobbed.

He steered her toward a quiet corner of the building's grand foyer and sank onto a padded bench beside her, rubbing gentle circles on her back. "It'll be easier to fix if you don't make too many mistakes right now. Take a few deep breaths, and really think about what you want to do before we rush off, okay?"

"You don't think I should go?" She wiped fresh tears from her cheeks. "They basically kicked me out."

"They're not thinking straight either." Bronson grimaced. He never spoke badly about his employers, who were really more like sons, but this time it seemed like he was struggling to hold his tongue. "They jerked back like a person who smashed their own thumb with a hammer because the very last thing they ever wanted was to hurt you."

"*They* didn't. Marty did. Well, until they dumped me."

She sniffled, her vanity overtaking her pain as her crying abated. "That's going to leave a hell of a mark."

"It doesn't have to." Bronson's mouth was set in a grim line. "Look, I think a lot of all four of you, and I don't want to see you screw things up, okay?"

Kari nodded. She appreciated that even if it meant having her ass handed to her.

"Just because they said some dumb shit doesn't mean you have to agree with them. You've turned tail before when things got rough and it only made the situation worse. Don't do that again. And maybe..." Bronson sighed then, as if he resented them for making him talk this much, especially about feelings.

"Maybe what?" she asked.

"Maybe they need someone to fight for them. To tell them that they matter beyond their money or their..." He cleared his throat. "Skills in bed. Maybe they need a woman who can put up with the shit that comes along with being theirs, including publicity and jealous assholes who want to tear them apart."

She scrunched her eyes closed. It was hard to do, but she tamped down the emotions they'd evoked in her to consider the underlying motivations for their actions. She figured her ability to put them first was the very definition of love. The harder she tried, the more she was able to ignore her own agony and consider theirs.

Damn it, Bronson was right.

Kari had nearly made the biggest mistake of her life and quit on the three men she loved when they needed her to stand and fight.

She must have taken a while to really consider Bronson's advice, because he scrubbed his hand over his face and started to stand up. "Come on. I have a place in mind. Once you're settled, I can go back and collect Andi if you want some support while you're there."

The moment he proposed it, Kari knew it was the absolute wrong thing to do.

Hell no. Running had only made things worse so far.

She was going to stay. Show her men who they belonged to and how much stronger they were when they were together.

"No thanks, Bronson." Kari didn't take the hand he held out to her.

"Wait, what?" He shook his head. "You're not going out there on your own. That's not even an option."

"No, it's not." The corner of her mouth kicked up in a sad smile then, one she wouldn't have believed possible even a few minutes ago. "Because I'm not leaving."

"Oh." He grinned. "Well, that's...good. Great."

"Thank you for helping me pull my head out of my ass." She put her hands on his shoulders, went up on her tiptoes, and kissed him on his grizzled cheek.

She would have sworn he was blushing when he stammered, "You're welcome."

Kari waved over her shoulder, then dashed to the elevator. What the hell had she been thinking, slinking away with her tail between her legs like that? No. No way. That was the old Kari. The one who ran. The one who hid. The one who blamed herself for shit other people did.

That's not who she was anymore.

Ford, Brady, and Josh had taught her better.

Now it was time she showed them exactly who they'd been messing around with.

Kari had no idea what she was going to say when she charged back inside their penthouse. That was probably for the best because her thoughts flew out of her head the moment she burst into the kitchen and saw Ford with a fistful of Josh's shirt and his hand raised.

"What the hell are you doing?" she shrieked, racing to put herself between them.

She stared at Ford's knuckles, which quickly fell away from the vicinity of her face. He froze, then stumbled backward, his handsome face twisted into a mask of disgust and shame.

"I...I don't know." He shook his head violently as if to clear it and then said. "Fuck. I lost it when I thought you were gone for good. I'm sorry."

Brady was at Josh's side, glaring at each of his partners in turn.

Score one for Bronson. They needed her to bring them together again.

"Did you forget something?" Brady asked.

"Yeah, this." Kari snatched the crumpled newspaper off the floor. She spread it out, unwrinkling it carefully so that she could really look at it for the first time. It was a gorgeous picture of them, making love with the twinkling lights of the city in the background.

If anyone who saw that was stupid enough to assume it meant she deserved what had happened to her with Marty, then they were idiots. She stroked the magazine lovingly. "I forgot to tell you that I'm not going to hide what we share. And that I don't give a shit who knows how much I love all three of you."

Josh looked up, completely confused. "You're not? You should care. Wait...you *what*?"

"Marty's already taken enough from me. He won't take you guys too." She crossed her arms and tapped her toe on the polished marble floor. It would be unjust to ask her to sacrifice the best thing in her life in order to punish the worst. She would take her chances.

"I'm tired of hiding and acting like what I want is wrong." Kari stood tall, the burden of her past lightening by the second as she embraced everything they'd given her. Everything they'd taught her about herself. "I want to be bolder. I want to be the woman worthy of three men like you."

"No one ever said you weren't." Brady reached for her, cupping her cheek. "I hope that's not how you interpreted our concerns."

Kari's eyes stung. It was hard to rein in the avalanche of emotions that had taken her for such a rollercoaster ride that morning and over the past several months. "I know you were thinking of my best interests, but it still felt like a rejection."

"It wasn't." Josh edged closer. He hugged her from behind, infusing her with his warmth and affection. "If anything, I don't feel worthy of you. I think you deserve more than to have your love life made into a freak show."

"Most people are lucky to find one person to spend their lives with. Here I am, with three. I mean, if that's what you want too..."

"Do you really mean that?" Ford stalked closer. "You're ready to take us on, along with all the bullshit that comes with being involved with us?"

"Yes. I can handle it." Kari stood straighter then. "It's going to take a lot more than someone showing the world how amazing we are together for me to bolt. I'm not leaving, not now and not ever."

"That's good, because we still have the potential to damage your case against Marty." Josh grimaced. "As much as I wish we could ignore that possibility, we can't.

Maybe we should hide that we're staying together. At least for now."

"Absolutely not. Here's the thing..." Kari drew a deep breath, hoping to sway three very logical, kick-ass lawyers with her argument. "The whole world has already seen that I sleep with you. What I want to show them is that it's so much more than that. It's a relationship. It's..."

Fuck, should she say it?

"What is it?" Ford asked.

"Love." There. It was out there. Hanging in between them. "Unconventional, yes. But definitely the most powerful love I've ever known."

Brady rushed to her and crushed her in a bear hug. "It is. For me too."

Josh and Ford were right behind him.

She was surprised to hear Josh chuckling. "You would have already known that, if you hadn't crashed from being so well-fucked last night."

"Seriously?" Her eyes widened.

"Yeah, we tried to tell you, but you were passed out." Ford kissed her temple, healing the last of the wounds they'd unintentionally inflicted earlier.

"So that should help my case, right? If I run...if people think all we did was have some kinky affair, *that* damages my chances. Instead, I want everyone to see that this is so much more. I mean...if it is for you too."

Josh pried her out of Brady's arms and smothered her in his own. He kissed her lightly, then said, "It is. I'm sorry, I shouldn't have let you walk out of here. I couldn't stand the thought that we could be harming you. You're right, though. That would only have made things worse. Not only for your trial, but because I don't want to live without you anymore."

Kari squeezed him back, afraid to let go. Because if she did, that meant she'd have to face Ford, and she knew he'd be the hardest to convince.

Brady and Josh flanked her as she turned toward him.

She was shocked to see him bent over, hands braced on his knees, his back heaving as if he was having trouble catching his breath or maybe trying not to cry.

Kari raced to him and rubbed his shoulder. "Hey, it's okay if you're not ready to commit. I know things have been changing fast. I understand if we're not all on the same page...yet."

"Kari..." He growled her name as if warning her to stop pushing. No way.

"Give this a chance. Please." She got angry again. "I'm not going to walk away from what I know has the potential to be the best thing in my life. Don't ask me to do that. Not if you care for me at all."

He bolted upright and shut her up by crushing his mouth over hers.

She lost track of time and place as he showed her exactly what he hadn't been able to put into words. A man couldn't touch her like that without an abundance of emotion to back up his caresses. She was sure of it.

When they finally broke apart for a breath, Ford said, "I love you and what we have together. I'm sorry I almost fucked it up for all of us."

She leapt at him, wrapping her legs around him as Brady and Josh surrounded them, pressing in on her from all sides. "However this turns out—with Marty, I mean—we know the truth. That is enough for me, as long as I have you."

Ford stared directly into her eyes when he said, "I will find a way to bring him to justice, whether that's through the courts or any other means needed to ensure you're protected. You have my word about that."

Kari didn't flinch. She didn't need to around him or Brady or Josh. They would never hurt her and would only elevate her further.

"We're going to battle this together," Brady promised her. Everything started falling back into place.

"No matter what happens, we'll be here for you," Josh vowed.

"Forever," Ford murmured.

The intensity of the moment might have devolved into some serious make-up sex if someone hadn't cleared their throat from the hallway.

23

"Please tell me everyone's got their clothes on," an exasperated Bronson called from the front entryway.

Kari laughed. If the guy had been a few minutes later, she figured the odds were good he might have gotten an eyeful. As it was, they'd barely had time to make up.

"All clear," Ford confirmed. "Come in. What's going on?"

"They got him." Bronson sported a smile the likes of which Kari had never seen on him. She was afraid his face might crack in half. "The cops were able to use the angle of the images published in the tabloid this morning to pinpoint his location. He'd rented an apartment in a building southeast of here so he could spy on you all. He's obsessed. The entire place was wallpapered in pictures of the four of you in every possible combination."

He didn't say they were naked in those snapshots. Still, Kari figured that was a reasonable assumption, especially when Bronson's stare slid carefully away from the grand piano on the other side of the room.

He continued, "Anyway, Marty's locked up and he's going to stay that way for a very long time."

"If we do our jobs right." Ford crossed his arms.

"I hate to disappoint you, but I don't think you're going to need to flex your lawyerly muscles in court." Bronson's grin widened even more. "One of the guys heading up the investigation is ex-military too. We have a few connections in common. Through them, I heard the bastard confessed. To a whole lot of shit. Including the assault of three other women, harassment of a half dozen more, and stalking Andi. The cops convinced him it was better to come clean and hope for leniency in a plea deal than letting you three take a swing at him."

"He always was smart. I'll give him that." Brady sighed.

Josh linked his fingers with Kari's. "How do you feel about that?"

"I honestly don't care. As long as he can't ruin anyone else's life, I'm happy." She smiled up at her three men and Bronson, who nodded at her.

"Congratulations," he said to them as he headed for the door.

Kari knew he was referring to a hell of a lot more than the Marty situation.

When they were alone again, Kari wandered over to the sectional and sank onto it. She wasn't sure if she wanted to do a victory lap around the enormous living area or sleep for a month. Compromising by some vigorous activity followed by a nap sounded like a good plan to her.

But it seemed the guys had another idea. Brady said, "You know, Marty isn't going to bother you ever again."

She nodded. "Thank God."

Ford took a deep breath, then said, "I guess what I'm

saying…" He cleared his throat once, twice, and looked at Brady. "Help me out. I can't do it. Can't bring myself to sabotage what we have going, not twice in one morning—"

Josh cut Ford off. "It needs to be said. Kari has choices and we respect them. This should be her decision."

Brady nodded, taking over. "Ford means that you don't have to stay here, with us, in order to be safe anymore."

"Oh." Kari winced. She turned her back to them and drifted toward the windows. She trailed her fingertips over the piano as she went, remembering all that had happened since this fiasco had started and how utterly her life had been altered.

How so many amazing and terrible things could be wrapped up together was hard for her to comprehend. They wouldn't blame her if she was confused about it all.

"Does that mean you're ready for me to move out? Go back home while we work on stuff between us?" She didn't look at them when she asked it, but the disappointment was clear in her voice no matter how hard she attempted to disguise it.

"Never." Josh rushed to her and put his hand on her shoulder. "We just want you to understand that you have options."

"The best of which would be if you make our home your home too," Ford said, ignoring dirty looks from Brady and Josh. "What? We only agreed we wouldn't force her to stay. But we didn't say anything about making our preferences known when this day came."

"You thought about this?" Kari couldn't say why that shocked her. They were careful planners. Strategists. Something that helped her feel secure with them.

"Yes," Brady told her. "And we have something we'd like to give you."

Ford strode over to a bookshelf and took a small box from one of the shelves along with an envelope.

"It's not a ring, so don't freak out. Okay?" Josh told her.

"If I had my way, it might have been." Ford stopped just short of scowling. "But they told me it's too soon for that and I shouldn't scare you away again."

Kari laughed. Considering that she'd nearly bolted less than an hour ago, she figured the guys were right. They weren't ready for that yet. So what could they have up their sleeves?

Brady and Josh shuffled closer as Ford handed her their gift. They waited patiently as she neatly unwrapped the bow.

She lifted a gold pen from the satin pillow cradling it. "Thank you, guys. It's beautiful."

"We're hoping you'll use it for a few really important things," Brady explained.

"Like...?" Kari tilted her head as she studied them, trying to figure out what they had in mind. There was no way she could guess, though.

Ford reached behind the chair. He'd stashed something there. When? It had to have been at least the night before since they'd been together nearly every moment since then. So this morning's fiasco hadn't spurred him to do this. They'd been planning it all along.

That thought took away some of the lingering jitters in Kari's stomach. "What is that?"

Brady explained, "Back in college, we made a list of all our goals. The big picture ones. And we've crossed them all off. You inspired us to add one and we think it's only fitting that you do the honors...you know, if we've succeeded."

The three guys circled around and let her read what it was they wanted so badly that only she could give them.

Convince the woman of our dreams to spend the rest of her life being worshipped by us.

Live the rest of our lives satisfied and happy.

Kari sniffled, then knuckled a tear from the corner of her eye. Damn it, they'd made her cry twice in one day. But how could she not when they were sweet, and sexy, and making all her dreams come true?

"It's okay if we haven't yet. We're not going to give up until we do." Josh puffed out his chest.

"No, it's not that. Of course you have. I just can't believe I'm the woman lucky enough to get to do this." Kari closed the gap between her and the paper Ford held out. With a flourish worthy of one of the signers of the Declaration of Independence, she put a big, bold check in the middle of the box.

Before they celebrated too much, Brady opened the envelope and withdrew a crisply folded sheet of paper, very different from the weathered to-do list. He flattened it out and handed it to her. "You can also use your pen to sign this."

"What is it?" Kari began to read, her eyes growing wider by the sentence.

"It's an offer letter," Josh told her. "We want to hire you again, with a huge promotion and a raise. Not because you sleep in our beds, but because the office is falling apart without you. Please, please come back."

Brady wasn't afraid to beg either. "You're the glue that holds us together. We need you. Please."

She looked to Ford. He nodded. "They're right. It's not the same without you."

Kari took her time, scanning their letter, which was more than fair, before she said, "On one condition…"

"Anything," Ford promised.

"You have to break the news to my boss. He's going to be pissed."

The guys laughed. Ford stuck out his hand and shook with her on it. "Deal."

Then he pulled her into a hug that he capped with a kiss, which turned into a makeout session between the three of them and another sexual escapade worthy of the tabloids.

24

Kari sighed as she watched Andi dance with Cooper, Simon, and Reed. They had their own way of moving together, their own rhythm that only they could see and feel. It was familiar and yet different from how she was with her men.

Andi looked stunning in the romantic, classic gown she'd chosen to wear to their wedding. It meant something to Kari that every detail, from Andi's antique ring to her dress to the ceremony and venue for the reception, felt very much like a traditional ceremony despite its very unconventional outcome.

In the six months since Kari had moved in with Ford, Brady, and Josh permanently, that had been her biggest concern. What if one day they realized it was too hard to prove what they'd set out to make clear to each other and the rest of the world—that they were in a committed, loving, *enduring* relationship?

So far they were making it work despite the extensive media coverage of the Marty drama, learning to work together again, and navigating the normal pitfalls of living with someone for the first time. If they did fight, there was always spectacular make-up sex to look forward to.

Kari hoped that one day it would be her beaming at her new husbands like Andi was that night.

When it was time for the bouquet toss, she reluctantly joined the other women in a huddle at the back of the room. She wasn't really the type to claw other ladies for a bundle of flowers or even the right to be married next, since she already had the men she wanted in her life and labels weren't really their thing.

It was easier to go along with the crowd and half-ass it than to object, so she rolled her eyes at Ford, then took her obligatory place in the herd of hopefuls.

Andi wound up, then launched her flowers as if she were the star pitcher in the World Series. The bouquet got tangled in the ceiling fan. It spun around and around before slingshotting directly at Kari's face.

It was grab the damn thing or take a thorn to the eye. She refused to tell that story over and over at the office next week, when people asked about the freak accident that had led to a temporary eye patch.

Her hand shot out reflexively, wrapping around the stems of the admittedly beautiful white roses. And next thing she knew, she was clutching the bouquet while everyone else in the room shrieked, clapped, and cheered. The photographer's flash nearly blinded her with a rapid-fire series of blasts worthy of a laser gun or a solar flare.

The photographer turned toward the rest of the guests and said, "Who's here with this lovely lady? Let me take a picture that you can display at your future wedding."

The room was filled with murmurs and Kari's own nervous, awkward chuckle. Hopefully the guys would be good sports. Her knees went weak when the three of them came forward. Shoulder to shoulder to shoulder, they cut through the crowd.

"Is this the sign you were waiting for?" Josh asked Ford as they neared.

Brady elbowed Ford and said, "Come on. It's perfect timing."

Ford grinned, then stepped forward. He glanced over his shoulder at their hostess. In a booming voice that projected through the reception hall as well as it did courtrooms, he said, "Andi, will you hate me forever if I steal the spotlight for a second?"

The bride jumped up and down, clapping. "Not if you're about to do what I think you are."

He saluted her and her new husbands before turning to Kari once more.

"What? Ford..." Kari's mouth hung open. Not very flattering for those pictures.

"It's my turn to speak." He shushed her as he sank to one knee.

Josh and Brady did the same, one on either side of him.

The three handsome men she loved with all her heart made a very public display as Ford fished in his pocket for a box that she knew for sure did not hold a pretty pen.

When he opened it, she gasped, her hand flying to her chest to try and contain her racing heart.

How could he even expect her to lift her arm if he put a rock that big on her finger?

They were about to find out.

Because he said simply, "Kari, we love you. We'd be honored if you'd be ours forever. Will you marry us?"

The moment she said yes and he slid that gleaming, ginormous, gorgeous ring on her finger, they were surrounded by friends. Andi, Cooper, Reed, and Simon piled on to their four-person embrace.

Kari glanced at her finger, then at the men she could officially call hers.

For keeps.

4-EVER THEIRS

JAYNE RYLON

NEW YORK TIMES BESTSELLING AUTHOR

If you missed out on the 4-Ever series, start with 4-Ever Theirs to find out how Andi hooked up with her three roommates in the first place.

One woman. Three dudes. No regrets.

College was supposed to be Andi Miller's training ground for the real world. Instead, it's her final Saturday night in her college-grade apartment, and she's still sheltered as hell. Why? Because of her three adorable roommates—Reed, Cooper and Simon.

Determined to have one date where the overprotective trio doesn't scare the guy off, Andi sneaks out for the night. And almost lives to regret it.

When Reed, Cooper and Simon rescue Andi from a bad situation in the basement of a sex club, they decide it's time for the kid gloves to come off. Since their early college days, they've been not-so-secretly fighting amongst themselves to spark her next smile, her next laugh.

They've already done a lot of surviving together, and now it's time to thrive. At the risk of ruining a beautiful friendship, the men set out to turn their hands-off live-in arrangement into a weeklong learning experience where they become Andi's sex education teachers.

Except none of them realize their new found intimacy will make it impossible to say goodbye on graduation day.

An Excerpt From 4-Ever Theirs:

"Stop. Stop. I'm going to pee my pants." Andi Miller gasped between bouts of hysterical laughter. She swiped tears from her cheeks as her three obnoxiously adorable roommates demonstrated their best attempts at twerking from various places around their kitchen.

Sadly, Simon could definitely shake his ass better than she could. He put on quite a show from his perch atop their rickety table, threatening to turn it into kindling with sharp swings of his hips. The guy could easily have paid his portion of the rent and then some if he'd gotten a job as a go-go dancer.

"We're only trying to help." Cooper punched Simon in the leg then grappled him to the floor. If she didn't act fast, this could deteriorate into another of their infamous wrestling matches. The last one of those had resulted in the annihilation of a beanbag chair. She was still discovering tiny foam beads scattered throughout their apartment months later.

"I mean, it's not like you've come out of your room long enough to pick up any of our moves in the past four years, with all that studying you insisted on doing. You don't want to get embarrassed on the floor tonight, do you?" Reed asked as he simulated humping a cabinet.

Well, that wouldn't be a problem, seeing as she hadn't quite told them the truth about her destination for the evening. Dance club, hook-up spot—same difference, right?

Their over-protectiveness made her white lie necessary.

Besides, she owed them the same courtesy they showed her when it came to keeping their sex lives separate from their home lives.

The guys never brought women to the apartment. Or at least they hadn't in ages. Not since early in the first semester of their freshman year when one of their one-night stands—to this day, they wouldn't tell her which of them had slept with the poor girl—had tried to make herself some morning-after breakfast and ended up with a black eye courtesy of Andi's fist.

Hey, how was she supposed to have known it wasn't an intruder out there whipping up a frittata before absconding into the night with their meager college-grade possessions? Milk crate furniture might be hot on the black market for all Andi knew. If some of the oomph propelling her swing had actually been fueled by jealousy instead of fear, she'd hidden that pathetic fact as best she could from both herself and her roommates.

Ruining their friendships wasn't on her agenda. She wasn't the sort of girl who knew how to screw around then act like sex had been no big deal. Though she had chemistry with each of her roommates, how awkward would it have been to have followed through on it and slept with one of them?

Takeout and movie nights with the others would never have been the same.

Andi admitted it. She was sheltered as fuck. Though her vocabulary had gotten a hell of a lot more colorful as a result of her co-habbing with this trio of idiots for the past four years, she hadn't done a lot of exploring relationship-wise. After all, she spent most of her free time with

Cooper, Reed and Simon. Who would approach her with those three hovering over her, snarling and baring their teeth at any guy who got too close?

God, she was going to miss them.

The thought of giving up their second-to-last Saturday night together had her rethinking her plans. Except this might be her last chance to eliminate her regrets about not having a single fling during her college experience. It would help round out her academic studies and the rewarding social experiment living with three dudes had turned out to be.

This was supposed to be her training ground for the real world.

Now that she'd accomplished the majority of her goals —by graduating at the top of her class and scoring a prime position in her field—maybe she could make some time to fill the emptiness growing inside her as she accepted that she'd be forging out on her own soon. The lack of a relationship hadn't bothered her so much when she'd had school and her roommates' friendship to occupy her.

All of that was changing.

So was she.

Andi wanted to be ready for what came next.

"Was it that good for you?" Simon flashed a wicked smile as he teased her.

"Huh?" She snapped herself out of her daze.

"Our dancing."

"Oh, yeah. Definitely. It was so hot I need to go take a shower." She rolled her eyes and giggled some more as she abandoned the kitchen for their shared bathroom. If she was sweating a little, it was surely from nerves over what she was about to do, not because they'd affected her.

Sure.

She scrubbed herself then spent a while drying and curling her hair before applying what dashes of makeup she owned—a bit of mascara and some nude lip gloss. The whole time, she kept wondering what tonight might be like if she could spend it with someone she knew and trusted instead of gambling on a blind date set up by her well-meaning chemistry lab partner.

Andi bit her lip then harrumphed and fixed the damage, at least mentally reminding herself not to rub her eyes before she could wreck them too. She sighed then rested her forehead on the door, praying for some direction. Was she making a mistake? Or would it be an even bigger one to pursue the foolish ideas tempting her to feel out her roommates about her proposition?

Before she could make up her mind, a rap on the door rattled her brains.

"Ouch. Fuck." She stumbled back.

"Yo, Andi. Quit hogging. I drank three beers with dinner, and I gotta piss," Reed groaned. "I forgot what it's like to wait on someone trying to be girly."

Aaaaaaaaand... That sealed the deal.

They were too much like brothers to ever see her as a woman. Which was exactly how she'd wanted things while they lived together. She grinned as she opened the door. Reed squashed past her in the doorway, wedging them together when he froze. "Damn.

Uh, you look...great."

"The magic of wearing something other than sweats and one of your roommates' old shirts sans a bra." She shrugged.

"I kind of prefer the no-bra part." Simon waggled his

193

brows from where he scarfed another helping of now-cold pizza for second dinner.

When she turned to him with a smile, he paused mid-bite.

"What?" Andi finger-combed her hair as she stepped from the bathroom so Reed could relieve himself in peace. Not that the guys didn't invade her privacy often when she was in the shower, or vice versa. The trials of a single bathroom for four people had absolutely played a part in her collegiate years.

"I told you," Reed shouted through the door.

"They're right. You're hot." Cooper took her hand and spun her around. "I'm not sure we should let you go out like this, young lady."

"Whatever, Dad." She chuckled until he finished twirling her, though it hadn't entirely been a joke. With her parents both gone, these guys had stepped up and filled a huge, painful void as best they could. They were, and always would be, her family.

In the heels Andi had borrowed, she was closer to Cooper's height. Meeting his warm stare, she caught the spark of something serious there.

Could he actually be attracted to her?

She knew each of them appealed to her in various ways—Cooper's gentlemanliness and tact, Simon's playfulness and daring, Reed's sense of responsibility and control.

As if a sliver of possibility was the only prompt her subconscious required, she blurted the thoughts that had been haunting her for the past hour. Okay, longer than that. At least since she'd agreed to this outing. Probably since the day she co-signed their lease.

"Maybe you guys should come out too?" She prided

herself on the fact that she only stammered a little when she said, "Or I could stay home and we could have a private party instead."

Simon blinked at her, the pizza still lodged half-inside his mouth.

Cooper's fingers tightened around hers. His other hand landed at her waist to steady her. But he didn't say anything.

The door opening behind her broke the moment, forcing them apart.

Reed emerged as the toilet finished flushing in the background. It was as if her silly dreams circled the bowl then vanished down their clanky pipes when he grimaced. "What's that? Don't back out now. You've been looking forward to tonight all week. It's about time you cut loose. On your own. You've earned this."

"Oh. Okay." If they noticed the tremble in her faux smile, they didn't call her on it.

Andi decided to quit fucking around. Playing a game where she didn't know the rules was a sure way to lose. Reed was right. She had to learn to stand on her own, without leaning on them. Because in a matter of days, they wouldn't be part of her everyday existence anymore.

Graduation was a week away.

Her new life, the one where she'd be a lab tech in a prestigious pharmaceutical research firm—one that didn't include her roommates—was calling.

"Go ahead. Have fun," Simon said around a mouthful of pepperoni. "Besides, we've already—"

Cooper cleared his throat, but it was too late. She realized they must have dates. Of course they did.

"Hey, you'll be fine," he promised. He looked away before adding, "You don't need us."

Andi swallowed around the lump in her throat. She took a step forward and then another before grabbing her wristlet and keys out of the bowl at the end of the countertop.

If she was going to do this, she couldn't linger. Otherwise, she'd never convince herself to leave.

"Be safe!" Reed shouted as she closed the door softly behind her, determined not to let the stinging of her eyes turn into real tears and screw up her mascara.

To keep reading **4-Ever Theirs, click here.**

WANT MORE MENAGE?

If you liked reading about this steamy non-traditional relationship, you should check out Nice & Naughty, another of Jayne's menage stories.

Can one man satisfy Alexa's appetites? Or will it take two?

After a disastrous lesson in heartache, Alexa Jones confines her adrenaline rushes to intense boardroom negotiations. Her legendary control cracks and she indulges in a high-octane encounter on the hood of her sports car. She never planned to see the enticing stranger again. When she finds herself across the boardroom table from him, there's suddenly more at stake than just her career.

Justin Winston got more than he bargained for on his summer drive, but he should have known nothing is ever that easy. He's met the woman of his dreams yet he doesn't know who she is. Luckily, he can always count on his practical brother for the things that matter, and this time is no exception. But, when a web of corporate espionage entangles them all, it's clear Justin isn't the only one who's fallen for their mysterious siren.

In Justin and Jason, Alexa finds something as unique and rare as the patent they will risk their lives to secure. The freedom to explore—and satisfy—the full range of her desires. From naughty to nice. Can Alexa accept the love of two men?

Warning: This story contains light bondage, anal play and smoking hot brothers for double the fun and double the trouble.

An Excerpt From Nice & Naughty:

"She's beautiful," he murmured reverently.

The car. He's talking about your car. She tried to convince herself, but the rationalization rang false. While he admired the convertible, something more arced between them. Attempting to shake off the unusual reaction inflaming her senses by focusing on her vehicle, Alexa stepped a little closer.

"I've done a lot of work on it."

"Can I touch her?" His implicit understanding of her dislike for people handling her vehicle made her confident he would treat it with the respect it deserved.

"Sure, go ahead." Plus, she got to watch the way his broad finger stroked the defined contour in the flawlessly waxed side panel, which inflamed her senses nearly as much as if he'd placed the caress on her skin instead.

Before she could stop to analyze what her subconscious offered, she asked, "Would you like to take a look under the hood?"

"Hell, yeah."

She had to laugh at the look on his face. "You look like a kid on Christmas."

"It's not every day I come across an opportunity like

this." The dark undercurrent of the statement and his piercing green stare made it clear he referred to more than a fancy sports car.

Oh God. He feels it, too.

Alexa should have been freaked out. Alone with a stranger, on a deserted stretch of highway, in the mountains far from the city, sounded like an unwise situation to put herself in. She should be nervous but a remarkable calm surrounded her instead. In fact, she just now realized she'd stopped on the side of the road without a second thought to safety. Today, she threw caution to the wind. The chemical reaction between them affected her like a drug.

As though he sensed her train of thought, the man backed away a few steps, displaying his non-threatening intent. He left the path clear for her to get in her car and drive away but her instincts shouted that she could trust him. She wanted to explore this attraction just a little bit further.

She leaned over the door and rested her fingertips on the hood release. The man's gaze tracked her movement yet he didn't encroach on her space. For a moment, the only sounds breaking the silence were the babble of the stream below, the gentle rustle of leaves from the tree branches overhead and a soft birdsong.

The air between them crackled with tension.

Then, the metallic click of the hood's latching mechanism disengaging relayed her decision to stay. A broad smile spread across his face, raising faint dimples that heightened his attractiveness. Alexa inclined her head in a "come here" gesture as she circled around to the front of the car.

He ambled to her side with a steady gait that made her

cognizant of his confidence she wouldn't run. Reaching for the edge of the hood simultaneously, their hands met. Sparks shot up her spine and she jerked. His arm wrapped around her waist in a protective hold. The solid strength kept her from losing her physical footing, but not her emotional balance. This close she could smell the unique combination of his leather gear and subtle, earthy cologne.

"Easy." His hand smoothed down her side and across the top of her ass as he went back to lifting the hood. The blatant touch imbued her with respect for his natural ability to handle a woman. However, she retained enough rationality to admire the gleaming chrome of the engine that she cleaned with painstaking diligence each weekend she could manage the time. Together they leaned forward, caught by the lure of a ridiculously overpowered motor.

"This is an aftermarket addition. Did you do this yourself?" His raised eyebrow conveyed his surprise.

"Yeah."

"I'm impressed. Are you a mechanic?"

"Nope, this is just a hobby." She smirked.

"Some hobby. I *am* a mechanic. This is a damn fine job."

Alexa basked in his appreciation for details. None of her friends understood her devotion to this machine. They couldn't comprehend why she spent the majority of her precious free time refining each tiny part until it was flawless. This man obviously did.

He ran his hand along the connections, searching with deft flicks of his fingertips for imperfections where none existed. His satisfied nod had her beaming.

"Jesus, woman. If someone told me I'd have the chance to play with a car like this today, I'd have said that nothing could distract me. But the way you're looking at me..."

His voice trailed off as she reached up to do a little exploring of her own. Her hand moved on autopilot, following her desire, cupping the side of his stubbled face.

Is this guy for real?

The wet heat of his lips on her palm rasped against her nerves, stronger than any dream. She whimpered as he turned his head to lick the center of her palm before catching the sensitive skin between her thumb and index finger in his teeth in a gentle nip. The move set her ablaze, destroying common sense.

"Kiss me," she demanded.

He didn't need to be told twice. With a low groan, he closed the narrow gap between them, sealing his mouth over hers. He dropped the hood in place and put his hand to better use, wrapping it around her hip, yanking her tight against the hard plane of his chest. His height made Alexa strain on tiptoes to return his kiss. Eager to help, he tucked his other hand around her thigh, just beneath the curve of her ass, and hoisted her up higher on his body.

They fit perfectly together.

Her hands tangled in his hair, loving the way the silky strands teased the sensitive crevices between her fingers. She kneaded his scalp, urging him to take her mouth deeper. His head angled over hers, intensifying the kiss as his tongue lashed playfully against the seam of her lips. She drew it inside her mouth and sucked. He tasted like peppermint.

She moaned with regret when he pulled away.

"I'm going to set you on the hood." He rumbled in her ear in between nibbles of her neck.

"No! Wait."

Though he looked disappointed, he stopped without hesitation.

The heat suffusing her face highlighted her discomfort with being so brazen. "I... I don't want to scratch the paint. Take my shorts off first."

Strained laughter burst from his chest. It transformed his features from rugged to unbearably handsome.

"Honey, you're my every fantasy."

To keep reading **Nice & Naughty, click here.**

NAUGHTY NEWS

Want to win cool stuff? Get sneak peeks of upcoming books? How about being the first to know what's in the pipeline or where Jayne will be making appearances near you? If any of that stuff sounds good then sign up for Jayne's newsletter, the Naughty News. She never shares you information, pinky swear!

www.jaynerylon.com/newsletter

WHAT WAS YOUR FAVORITE PART?

Did you enjoy this book? If so, please leave a review and tell your friends about it. Word of mouth and online reviews are immensely helpful and greatly appreciated.

JAYNE'S SHOP

Check out Jayne's online shop for autographed print books, direct download ebooks, reading-themed apparel up to size 5XL, mugs, tote bags, notebooks, Mr. Rylon's wood (you'll have to see it for yourself!) and more.
www.jaynerylon.com/shop

LISTEN UP!

The majority of Jayne's books are also available in audio format on Audible, Amazon and iTunes.

GET IN TOUCH

Jayne Loves To Hear From Readers
www.jaynerylon.com
contact@jaynerylon.com

ALSO BY JAYNE RYLON

4-EVER

A New Adult Reverse Harem Series

4-Ever Theirs

4-Ever Mine

EVER AFTER DUET

Reverse Harem Featuring Characters From The 4-Ever Series

Fourplay

Fourkeeps

POWERTOOLS

Five Guys Who Get It On With Each Other & One Girl. Enough Said?

Kate's Crew

Morgan's Surprise

Kayla's Gift

Devon's Pair

Nailed to the Wall

Hammer it Home

More the Merrier *NEW*

HOT RODS

Powertools Spin Off. Keep up with the Crew plus...

Seven Guys & One Girl. Enough Said?

King Cobra

Mustang Sally

Super Nova

Rebel on the Run

Swinger Style

Barracuda's Heart

Touch of Amber

Long Time Coming

HOT RIDES

Powertools and Hot Rods Spin Off.

Menage and Motorcycles

Wild Ride - Coming Soon!

Slow Ride - Coming Soon!

Rough Ride - Coming Soon!

Ride - Coming Soon!

Ride - Coming Soon!

MEN IN BLUE

Hot Cops Save Women In Danger

Night is Darkest

Razor's Edge

Mistress's Master

Spread Your Wings

Wounded Hearts

Bound For You

DIVEMASTERS

Sons Of The Compass Brothers Fall In Love

Heaven on Earth

Into the Fire

Still Waters

Light as Air

PLAY DOCTOR

Naughty Sexual Psychology Experiments Anyone?

Dream Machine

Healing Touch

RED LIGHT

A Hooker Who Loves Her Job

Complete Red Light Series Boxset

FREE - Through My Window - FREE

Star

Can't Buy Love

Free For All

PICK YOUR PLEASURES

Choose Your Own Adventure Romances!

Pick Your Pleasure

Pick Your Pleasure 2

RACING FOR LOVE

MMF Menages With Race-Car Driver Heroes

Complete Series Boxset

Driven

Shifting Gears

PARANORMALS

Vampires, Witches, And A Man Trapped In A Painting

Paranormal Double Pack Boxset

Picture Perfect

Reborn

PENTHOUSE PLEASURES

Naughty Manhattanite Neighbors Find Kinky Love

Taboo

Kinky

Sinner